OTHER YEARLING BOOKS YOU WILL ENJOY

THE KING OF MULBERRY STREET

DONNA JO NAPOLI

A YEARLING BOOK

Published by Yearling, an imprint of Random House Children's Books
a division of Random House, Inc., New York

Cover photograph: detail from *Mullen's Alley, Cherry Hill*.
Museum of the City of New York, The Jacob A. Riis Collection.

Yearling and the jumping horse design are registered trademarks
of Random House, Inc.

Visit us on the Web! www.randomhouse.com/kids
Educators and librarians, for a variety of teaching tools,
visit us at www.randomhouse.com/teachers

ISBN: 978-0-553-49416-7

Reprinted by arrangement with Wendy Lamb Books

Printed in the United States of America
July 2007
20   19   18   17   16   15   14   13   12
First Yearling Edition

ACKNOWLEDGMENTS

Thanks to Professor Umberto Fortis of the Archivio Renato Maestro in Venice for allowing me access to the materials about the history of Jews in Italy and for discussing them with me and recommending other readings. For comments on earlier drafts, thanks to Paolo Asso, Carolynn Laurenza, Paolo Munson, Helen Plotkin, Richard Tchen, Jeff Wu, and my editorial team: Suma Balu, Jack Lienke, Alison Meyer, and, especially, Wendy Lamb. Thanks also to Mary Reindorp's eighth-period sixth-grade language arts class at the Strath Haven Middle School in 2003–2004. And, as always, thanks to my faithful family.

But most most most of all, thank you to Thad Guyer, whose insights put me back on emotional track.

To Thad Guyer and the spirits of my grandfathers

THE KING OF
MULBERRY STREET

CHAPTER ONE

Surprise

I woke to Mamma's singing in the kitchen.

I pulled the sheet off my head. Mamma had tucked it over me to keep out mosquitoes and malaria.

The room was stifling. I got up from my bed of two chairs pushed together and opened the shutters. I straddled the windowsill, one leg dangling out, and savored the fresh air.

In the alley below, mothers hurried along on errands. I hoped someone would see me—the brave boy on the sill—so I could wave. A child from the market walked beneath me with a basket of flat beans on his head. They looked good.

There was a saying that no one starved in farmlands. My city, Napoli, was surrounded by farmlands, yet we'd been hungry for months. People went to bed trying not to think of food. Maybe Mamma sang to ward off that empty feeling.

I looked back into the room at Uncle Aurelio and Aunt Sara's bed. Baby Daniela's cradle sat on the floor. Aunt Rebecca, a widow, and my little cousins Luigi and Ernesto slept in another big bed.

Uncle Vittorio snored in the cot farthest from the kitchen, our other room. He cleaned streets, a night job, and slept by day.

I was nine, the oldest child in our home. Before I was born, a diphtheria outbreak killed all the other children and one aunt. So our friends celebrated at my birth. My grandmother, Nonna, told me they roasted a goat. They celebrated even though Mamma had no husband and I was illegitimate.

Nonna was the tenth person in our home. In winter we crowded into the kitchen to sleep around the oven, but the rest of the year the kitchen was Nonna's at night. Her cot was beside the credenza with the mirrored doors and lion feet that my grandfather had carved. She said his spirit lived in it, and she slept in the kitchen to be near him.

She also slept there so she could protect our home. She was tiny, but she knew dozens of charms against evil.

Now Baby Daniela made gulping noises. Aunt Sara scooped her from the cradle with one arm and rolled onto her side to nurse.

I got down from the window and walked into the kitchen to find warm bread on the table. Mamma kissed me, her anise-seed breath mixing with the smell of the bread. "Beniamino, *mio tesoro*—my treasure." She fit my yarmulke on my head and we said prayers. Then she tore a hunk off the loaf for me. I chewed in bliss.

Nonna's slow footsteps came up the stairs and I ran to open the door. She handed me a full basket of clothes.

Mamma got up in surprise. "For Sara?"

"And you," said Nonna with reproach in her voice.

Mamma wiped a drop of coffee from her bottom lip. "I'm going to find an office job," she said in a flat tone. "Soon someone will hire me. Then you'll all be glad."

"Magari," said Nonna. It was one of her favorite words. It meant *if only that were true.* "In the meantime . . ." She jerked her chin toward the basket.

Aunt Sara took in clothes for mending. At least, she used to; lately it seemed that people couldn't afford it. She'd be happy for this pile of work.

Mamma motioned to me to set the basket under the table. "How did you collect so much?" she asked Nonna.

"I was early and beat the competition."

"You don't have to go out that early," said Mamma. "You don't have to work so hard at your age."

"Magari." Nonna dropped onto a bench with an "oof." "Maybe I'll crochet today."

Nonna made baby clothes to sell at Hanukah and Christmas. It was my job to keep her yarn balls in order, piled just right. I went toward the yarn cabinet.

Mamma caught my arm. "Get ready. We're going out." Her smile surprised me; the night before I'd heard her crying quietly in the dark.

I raced into the corridor, to the water closet we shared with the neighbors on our floor. When I came back, I heard Nonna say, "Give up this idea of an office job. No doctor or lawyer will hire an unwed mother—and a Jewess, at that—to greet clients and keep records. You should work in a restaurant, cleaning up."

Mamma said, "You don't know. People will appreciate how well I read if they'll only give me a chance."

They hushed when I came in, as though they thought I didn't know it was my fault Mamma couldn't get an office job. But right now that didn't upset me. Mamma was in a good mood and errands were fun.

I pulled my nightshirt off and Nonna folded it, while Mamma held out my day shirt and pants to step into. As we went through the doorway, Mamma's fingertips grazed the box mounted on the doorframe that held the *mezuzah*. She boosted me up so I could touch it, too, though I scarcely looked at it. I didn't need its reminder—for I knew the Most Powerful One was unique and perfect.

Our alley opened onto the Via dei Tribunali, full of merchants and buyers and laborers on their way to work.

Men hooted obscenely and called things to Mamma as we passed. This happened to any woman alone; the prettier she was, the worse it got. Mamma was beautiful, so I was used to this. But I still hated it. Heat went up my chest. Even nine-year-olds knew those words. I glanced up at her, wanting to apologize for not being big enough to make them stop. But she didn't seem offended; she never did. She neither slowed down nor sped up, her leather-shod feet making quick slaps, my bare ones silent.

Mamma pointed at a small boy in the Piazza Dante. "That's Tonino's son," she said. "Tonino just sent money in a letter from America."

That spring, Tonino had left for America, where everyone got rich. "Good," I said. "Will they join him there now?"

"Not yet. He hasn't made much money." Mamma's hand tightened around mine. "But he will. He works in a coal mine."

We turned left down the wide Via Toledo. Gold numerals on black marble over the doorways told when the fancy shops were founded. Through glass windows I saw carved picture frames and chandeliers and shiny dresses. We passed a store filled with artificial roses, camellias, carnations, dahlias.

Mamma hesitated at the flower shop. I smiled up at her, but she stared at nothing, as though she was about to weep. Then she turned quickly and moved on. "Watch where you walk," she said.

The streets were dangerous for my bare feet. I looked down.

Mamma went into a cobbler's. That was odd; we never bought outside our neighborhood. From the doorway I peered into the cool dark. She talked to a man at a workbench cutting leather with giant scissors. He hugged her. She wrested herself free and beckoned to me. The man shook my hand and went into a back room.

Mamma called, "Wrap them, please. They're a surprise."

A surprise? I perked up.

"Come look first," he answered. "It'll only take a minute."

I waited while she went into the back.

She came out carrying a parcel wrapped in newsprint, tied with yellow string. The man handed me a licorice.

We continued down Via Toledo. I watched that surprise package. Mamma held it in the hand farther from me, and when I changed to her other side, she shifted the package to her other hand. It became a game, both of us laughing.

Mamma turned right, toward our synagogue. Napoli had only one synagogue and no Jewish neighborhood. Uncle Aurelio said the Jews of Napoli were the world's best-kept secret. The Spanish had kicked them out centuries before. But no matter how many times they were kicked out, they always snuck back.

We were as proud of being Jewish as of being Napoletani. My cousins were named after famous Jews: Luigi after Luigi Luzzatti, a Venetian and the first Jewish member of the House of Parliament; Ernesto after Ernesto Natan, one of Roma's most important businessmen. Uncle Aurelio lectured us cousins on the possibilities—*le possibilità*. "You can do anything if you put your heads to it and work hard. It doesn't matter what adversity comes; we are Jews—Napoletani Jews. We never miss a beat."

At the Piazza dei Martiri I climbed over the fence onto the back of a stone lion. Other kids' mothers didn't let them. But Mamma said that if the city didn't want kids playing on the lions, they shouldn't make statues just the right size for climbing on.

We turned down the alley A Cappella Vecchia and into the courtyard. Napoli's buildings were mostly three or four stories high. Around this courtyard, though, the buildings had five floors. Passing under the thick stone arch, I felt as though we were leaving the ordinary and coming into someplace truly holy.

"I love this courtyard," I said.

Mamma stopped. "More than you love the synagogue itself?"

I didn't want to answer. Maybe my preference for the openness of the courtyard meant there was something lacking in my soul.

She squatted, put a pinch of anise seeds in my palm, and looked up into my face as I chewed them. "Stand here and think of why you love this place. Then go spend the day doing exactly what you want." She straightened up.

"What do you mean?" Usually my family needed me to run errands.

"Visit all your favorite places. And, please, visit Uncle Aurelio and Aunt Rebecca at work." She put her hands on my cheeks. "I don't have money for you. But don't go home to eat at midday, because if you do, Nonna or Aunt Sara might give you a chore. No chores today. See Napoli. See all that you love."

I nodded in a daze of happiness. I would visit Aunt Rebecca at midday. She was a servant to a rich family and she always snuck me meat from their table.

"Stay well. You know how to be careful. I'll see you at dinnertime." She kissed my forehead. "Stay well, *mio tesoro.*"

CHAPTER TWO

Dirty

As I walked, children passed me on their way to school. I didn't go to school; Uncle Aurelio didn't like how Catholic teachers put religion into the lessons. So he taught me numbers and Mamma taught me reading. Mamma said I needed more than that and I was smart enough not to let the Catholic teachers influence me. She had just about talked Uncle into letting me go to school in autumn.

Crowd noises came from Via Toledo. I ran over to see men in gloves and top hats and horses in black cloth hoods with white rings around their eyeholes marching down the road. A funeral. A flag waved the family crest from the top of the coach that carried the women in the dead person's family. It must have been someone important.

The casket rolled by with lilies on top. Lilies in

summer. Somehow Catholic funerals had real lilies, no matter the season. If only I could take one—just one—for Mamma.

I made my way to the next road, where I begged a ride from a horse-drawn cart to the stables where Uncle Aurelio worked.

He smiled when I came in, but we didn't speak. He was scraping the rear hoof of a mare. When he finished, Uncle Aurelio walked outside with me. "So what's the message? Who sent you?"

"I just wanted to see you. I'm on my way up the hill."

"To Vomero?" He winked. "Going to snitch food from the midday meal?" He put his hand on my head, in the center of my yarmulke. The weight made me feel solid and safe.

I climbed onto the next cart going toward Vomero. At the base of the hill, I took the stairs up to the piazza and looked down and out over my town and the bay and the two humps of Mount Vesuvio beyond. The buildings shone yellow and orange, and the bay sparkled green, dotted with fishing boats and merchant boats and sailboats. A huge steamer docked in the port. I saw bright market umbrellas in piazzas, and a train slowing to a halt at the station, and oxen pulling carts on the bay avenue.

I turned to face the wide Vomero streets with sidewalks under the wispy fringe of acacias. A couple strolled along, arms linked. Everything was calm—so different from the Napoli below. Vomero was rich; rich people didn't have to hustle all the time. The people here owned the sailboats on the bay. The women played tennis in white dresses to their ankles, with sleeves to their knuckles; the men cheered for their sons at soccer matches. Their lives were a mystery of leisure.

A boy sat on a barrel beside a cow and filled pails with milk for servants to carry back to the big, airy houses. Aunt Rebecca stood waiting. When her pails were full, I carried one while she carried the other.

Aunt Rebecca was not lovely like Mamma or Nonna. Everyone had been delighted when she got married and devastated when her husband was killed in a street fight. No one expected her to remarry. But her looks were in her favor when it came to being a servant. Rich women didn't hire pretty servants; their husbands might like them too much.

Entering the house, I heard the noises of *tombola*— bingo—from the parlor. Aunt Rebecca went on to the kitchen, but I stopped and peeked.

"Look." One of the three girls on the sofa pointed at me.

I stepped back into the hall, out of sight.

"It's just a servant's boy," said a second girl.

"Make him play with us."

"He's dirty."

I wasn't dirty. Or not that dirty.

"It's more fun with more people. Get him, Caterina."

We played *tombola* at home, like every Napoli family. But what boy would play with girls? I hurried to the kitchen and set the milk pail on the counter. Aunt Rebecca looked sideways at me from her chopping. I put a finger to my lips and ducked behind the pantry curtain.

"Where's your nephew?" came Caterina's voice.

"I thought there was a noise on the cellar steps," said Aunt Rebecca. Not a lie—just a crafty answer.

"Why would he go down there?"

"I could use a bucket." More craftiness.

I heard steps cross the room. "Are you down there, boy?" Caterina called. "Come on up. We want you."

I burst from the pantry and ran out the front door. I didn't stop to pant till I reached the bottom of the hill. Stupid me, now no lunch.

I passed the window where Nicola sold hot, almond-speckled *taralli*—dough loops. My mouth watered, my stomach fluttered.

Oh, for a coin to buy a dough loop.

Instantly, I thought of the convent. I set off running to the church of San Gregorio Armeno and clanked the iron knocker on the side chapel door.

My favorite nun answered. "Ah, Beniamino, what a pleasure." She kissed my cheeks. "What brings you here?"

"Perhaps you might need help?"

"Of course. You're getting bigger. You should help us more often while you can still fit through the passageways. Come."

I followed her to the floor hatch that opened to the ladder down to the grotto. She put a key in a pouch, then added a backup candle, two matchsticks, and rough paper. She hung the pouch around my neck and gave me a candle. "Two bottles today."

That might mean double pay. I held the lit candle sideways between my teeth and went down the ladder. Twenty-two rungs. That was nothing. Some grottos were two hundred steps down.

The grottos and the channels between them formed the ancient water system, connected to the old aqueducts aboveground. Greek slaves had built it a thousand years before. The grottos had been closed for nearly a century, but they were still used as wine cellars; and thieves climbed down them, then crawled up old, dry wells into the atriums of fancy homes when the people were out. I'd never seen a thief here, but other boys claimed they had.

Once I saw a lover, though. Lovers of rich married women came and left like thieves. I knew the man was a lover, not a thief, because he smiled as we passed. A boy told me lovers came to the nuns, too. But they couldn't come to my nuns—not unless they were as small as I was—because of the awful tunnel.

At the bottom of the ladder I took off my yarmulke and left it safely under the last rung. I followed the passageway to where the ceiling came down so low I had to crawl. I held the end of the candle in my mouth now, so that the flame led the way. The walls were wet from the humid air. My hair stuck to my neck.

I'd gone through this tunnel many times, but it always seemed endless. I was afraid I'd die there.

Then suddenly I was out. I stood and breathed, and oh, what was that terrible smell? Something lay in the channel ahead. I held out my candle to see better. A body! I screamed and the candle fell. I crawled to the wall. I sat and pulled my feet up quick under my bottom. I wedged the backup candle between my knees and struck a match on the rough paper. The flame fizzled out and the dark swallowed me. My hands were wet from the damp air, so I blew on them frantically. I struck the other match; it flamed and the wick took. Blessed light.

I pressed my back against the wall and stood on tiptoe to look again. Rats ripped at the naked, bloated body of a man.

My eyes burned. The month before, an old man had stabbed a man on our street. A week later a young man had shot another in the piazza. When the stabbing happened, I was with Mamma. She whisked me home and held me till I slept. For the shooting, I was alone. I bit my knuckles to keep from screaming. The shooter walked up to me, and I recognized him—he lived nearby. He knocked my yarmulke off with the tip of the gun and hissed, "*Bastardo* Jew." *Bastardo*—a name for mongrel dogs, not people.

I ran home, but I didn't tell Mamma. She would have cried. I didn't cry then and I battled away tears now. Boys didn't cry.

I kept my eyes straight ahead till I got to the locked grotto that held the convent's special wines. I took two bottles and walked back. Fast, fast past the body. Hardly breathing.

At the tunnel I tried to tuck the bottles into my waistband. They wouldn't both fit. The idea of leaving one behind and passing through that tunnel two more times to fetch it was unbearable. So I lay on my back in the tunnel with my hands cradling the bottles on my belly and with the candle in my mouth. Little by little I scooched headfirst the length of that tunnel, as hot candle wax dripped on my chest through my open collar.

When I got to the ladder, I kissed my yarmulke and stuck it on my head. I climbed up with one bottle and put it on the convent floor, then went down for the other before I could think twice. I set it beside the first, crawled out, and stood.

"What's the matter, child? You smell awful."

The nun's worried face undid me; I cried. Loudly, as

though I was crying for everyone who had ever died and everyone who ever would. And I thanked the Most Powerful One that there were only nuns to watch me disgrace myself like this.

Soon five nuns huddled around me, wiping me with a wet cloth, offering water and bread with chocolate. I rinsed my mouth. "There was a body," I said.

"Oh. That. Ah." My favorite nun smoothed my hair gently. None of them was surprised. The cemeteries were full, so after funerals, men dug up the corpses and dumped them in the grottos.

I ate as they talked. Chocolate, such good chocolate, speckled with nuts.

My favorite nun lifted the pouch from my neck. "A candle is missing." She touched my cheek. "Munaciello stole it."

Munaciello was a spirit who hid things. Children blamed him, not adults. I felt charmed, though her words were just kindness, to keep the head nun from charging me for that candle.

The head nun gave me three coins. Three! "Beniamino, special one." She was about to tell me to become Catholic. Mamma hated my coming here because of that. But for three coins, let her blab. Besides, she called me special. Everyone said my cousins Luigi and Ernesto were special because they were named after famous men, but only Mamma thought I was special. "A boy with no earthly father is always special," said the nun. "Jesus Christ was just so. Your right place is here, child."

Despite the praise, I knew she felt sorry for me; I was Jewish and fatherless. What a fool she was to feel that way.

Being Jewish was best. And Nonna had taught me not to be jealous of children with fathers. *"Chi tene mamma, nun chiagne"*—Whoever has a mother doesn't cry. A proverb. That's all I needed, all anyone needed: a mother.

My favorite nun handed me half a lemon dipped in sugar. "That extra coin can't lessen the horror behind, but it may make the prospects ahead better, right?" That was why she was my favorite—she spoke straight. "Come back soon, sweet one."

I sat on the step and blinked at the sunlight. The lemon made my mouth fresh, but I couldn't shake the feeling of being dirty. The odor of the corpse clung to me.

I walked slowly through the empty streets; people had gone home for the afternoon rest. The three coins pressed into my fist. I needed something to put them in so I wouldn't lose them.

I took a side street, where a girl sat on a chair outside while her mother combed her hair. At the next corner a woman dressed in rags picked lice from the head of a boy at her feet. They were all poor. Maybe poorer than us.

I came out into the marketplace. In front of an oil store a family had set out a table under a canopy of grapevines. Their meal was over, but two men leaned back in their chairs, talking.

A fine gentleman came into the square, and a man and two boys appeared from nowhere. The man plunked down a shoe-shine box and the gentleman put a foot up on the box. One boy stood behind the gentleman and reached a stealthy hand under the loose hem of his fancy coat. He pulled out a handkerchief and stuffed it under his own shirt.

The thief looked hard at me.

The man finished the shoe shine, and he left with the boys.

People were robbed all the time; still, I went all jittery.

My family would hit me if I stole. Nonna especially. She'd recite: *"Chi sparagna 'a mazza nun vô bene ê figlie"*— Those who don't beat their children don't love them. Then she'd hit me again. And the Most Powerful One, He'd never forgive me.

The men at the table were still talking. Had they noticed? I'd noticed, but the thief had glared at me to make sure I'd never tell. Like the man with the gun who'd said, *"Bastardo* Jew."

I felt dirtier than ever. In the trash I spied a matchbox. I slipped the coins into the box and tied the ends of my pant strings around it, then tucked it in at my waist. Now to get clean.

I ran along the bay to a cove. Boys were jumping off a fishing boat. They were naked, like most boys at the beach, but these boys were probably always naked except in church. They were *scugnizzi*—urchins, the poorest of the poor. No one trusted them. One stood on the gunwale and jabbed with a pole under the water. A seagull circled, screeching greedily.

They didn't look at me, but they knew I was there. They were aware of everything that happened; *scugnizzi* always were. If I hid the matchbox, it would disappear while I was swimming.

I was so filthy. I had to swim. Where else could I go?

Vesuvio, of course. Up to the rain-filled craters near the volcano's peak. I hitched a ride on the coastal road and lay on my back in the empty wagon, arms and legs spread wide. The sides were high; I saw only clouds. The air smelled of sea. I felt tiny—a speck of nothing, suspended without time or care.

The wagon turned inland and stopped in front of the monastery at the base of Vesuvio. Then I climbed on foot.

Some of the crater lakes were so hot they bubbled. I stopped at the first one that wasn't steamy, and I hid the matchbox under a rock. Then I took off my clothes, swished them in the water, and stretched them to dry on a rock while I swam. The water was heavy like oil and stank of sulfur. I scrubbed my skin nearly raw with bottom silt, the black volcanic ash.

When I came out of the water, my pants were gone. I had two pairs—one for the Sabbath, one for other days. Now one was gone. But the matchbox was undisturbed.

In my wet shirt I walked with slow, heavy steps downhill. Mamma would be furious, Nonna would smack me, my uncles would shout. It wasn't that I was indecent; my shirt came to my knees. But how much did pants cost? And I was supposed to be smart; no one should have been able to steal from me.

It was late by the time I got to the coastal road and hitched a ride on a cart. When I finally jumped off, I ran to the kosher butcher. I bought three coins' worth of liver, for couscous, a rare treat, and raced home, where Mamma burst into tears and hit me on top of the head.

"Eh," said Nonna, *"E figlie so' piezze 'e core"*—Children are pieces of your heart. She smacked me on the back of my head.

"Your uncle is searching the streets for you," said Aunt Rebecca. "Instead of eating. You had us sick with worry."

Ernesto pointed at my legs and laughed. Luigi joined in.

"Your pants," said Uncle Aurelio. "What happened?"

I shrugged and avoided his eyes.

The room smelled of tripe. I lifted my nose and sniffed.

"Your foolish mother spent a fortune on a feast," said Aunt Sara, nursing Baby Daniela. "And you didn't even show up."

I held out my bundle, a silent plea for forgiveness, and the women went into action. Aunt Rebecca minced the liver, Nonna peeled onions, Mamma grated old bread for the meatballs. They had to cook the meat now, or it would spoil.

"You're just like your mother," said Aunt Sara. "It's stupid to sell your pants for money for meat."

"I didn't," I mumbled. "It was a thief. I went swimming."

"Scugnizzi." Nonna threw up her hands.

Aunt Sara sighed. "You know better than to swim without a friend to guard your clothes."

"He couldn't help it; Munaciello robbed him." Mamma smiled and I smiled back in grateful surprise. "We'll leave the dishes in the sink tonight. Munaciello needs something to eat."

"You just want to get out of work," said Aunt Sara. "Munaciello never eats when we leave the dishes dirty overnight."

"He's a spirit," said Mamma. "He eats the spirit of the food, not the food itself."

"You think you're too good for menial tasks."

"Enough," said Uncle Aurelio. He wagged his finger at the meat. "So where'd you get the money?"

"The nuns. I did a chore."

"The church is rich." Uncle Aurelio winked. "Next time be here for dinner. With your pants on. Now eat."

I filled my bowl with thin tripe slices and soft beans and ate greedily.

Nonna dumped hot meatballs into a bowl. She pointed toward the door with her chin, telling me to bring them to the Rossi family next door. If you received unexpectedly, you had to give unexpectedly. It was how friends behaved.

I delivered the meatballs, then raced back.

Uncle Vittorio came in only seconds behind me. "Ah, you're home, Beniamino," he said. "Now I can eat and go to work."

Mamma wiped sweat from her brow and raked her fingers through her hair. "Beniamino and I will sleep in here tonight. Nonna will sleep in my cot." Before Nonna could protest, Mamma put up her hand. "We'll guard this home with our lives."

So I lay on my chairs in the hot kitchen as Mamma whispered stories to me. I don't know which of us fell asleep first.

Once in the night I woke to Mamma's almost silent crying. Her back was to me, and her shoulder barely moved in the moonlight. I put my hand between the wings of her shoulder blades and pressed. She stopped, as she had the night before and the night before that. When we woke, I'd ask her what was wrong.

CHAPTER THREE

Shoes

I woke to Mamma's hand over my mouth. "Don't say anything," she whispered in my ear. "Don't make noise."

She dressed me in my synagogue pants and shirt. I loved those pants; they had pockets. And the shirt didn't have a single mended spot. She lingered over the buttons. I raised my hand to help and she firmly pushed it away. Then she sat me on the kitchen bench and put socks on my feet. Socks. And then, miracle of miracles, shoes. My first pair of socks, my first pair of shoes. That was what she'd had in that package the morning before. The big surprise. I stared through the faint dawn light and wiggled my toes. If I held them up, they just grazed the leather, there was so much room. The smell was heavenly: clean leather. Shoes got passed from the rich down to the poor. They always held a bump here from the first owner, a dent there from the second, scuffs along the toes from the third. But these were absolutely new—all mine.

She tied the laces in a bow and whispered, *"Antifurto,"* and with the two bow loops she made an extra knot against thieves.

From beyond the door came the muffled sounds of sleep. I wished the others were awake to see my shoes. Especially Luigi and Ernesto. It was all I could do to stay quiet.

I put on my yarmulke, took Mamma's hand, and walked proudly out the door. She lifted me and we touched the *mezuzah* together.

Though she hurried me, I walked carefully. I tried to make sure that nothing would dirty my shoes. It was hard because the light was feeble, the ground was covered with trash, and we walked fast. I kept imagining Luigi's and Ernesto's reactions. I would take care of these shoes so that they could be passed like new to Luigi.

The leather-smacking sound of my own footsteps was a surprise. The strangeness of walking on the street without feeling it underfoot almost made me laugh. Gradually, though, the giddiness wore off and I looked around.

The people out and about so early were mostly men who worked the farmlands. They had to walk an hour or two to reach their jobs. They carried bread in one hand and, if they were lucky, cheese in the other, eating as they went.

I smelled the sharp pecorino and wanted it. Without songs filling me as I woke, I was hungry. That morning Mamma hadn't sung. She'd acted as if we were sneaking out, on a secret treat.

The tenseness of her shoulders told me she was excited. I squeezed her hand in happiness. "Did you get a job?" I asked. "In an office? Are you starting today? Am I helping you?"

Mamma looked at me, her eyelids half lowered. "They hired someone else." Her voice broke.

I squeezed her hand again. "You'll get the next job."

She gave a sad "humph." Then she pulled me faster, the long shawl over her head and shoulders flapping behind. In this hot weather no one but an old crone would cover her head. Mamma must have been sweltering.

"Mamma, where are we going?"

She gripped my arm and pulled me along even faster through neighborhoods I'd never been in before. Long strands of spaghetti hung from poles in front of a pasta factory. Men dressed only in towels around their waists set more poles of pasta to dry in the sun. Other men wrapped dried strands in blue paper. Shopkeepers swept steps and washed windows before opening. The air was coffee. Men came out of coffee bars with powdered-sugar mustaches, licking pastry cheese from their teeth.

A group of women stood around an empty washtub and looked at us. Mamma snatched my yarmulke and tucked it inside her shawl. Why? Those women hadn't said anything. But Mamma's face was flushed.

The seagull screams grew louder. The first fishermen had already returned to the beaches near the port. They gutted fish and threw the innards to the swooping birds. A stooped man grilled fish tails for sale. My mouth watered.

Mamma stopped, as though she had heard my stomach call out. She ran onto the sand and talked to the man. He fashioned a cone from newsprint and filled it with fish tails. He squeezed on lemon and laced them with salt.

Mamma whispered a prayer and we squatted side by side. Normally, we'd sit to eat, like any Jew; we weren't horses. But there was nowhere clean. The Most Powerful One would understand—squatting was almost sitting. Mamma draped her shawl over my head, too, and we ate. Those fish tails were amazing.

I chewed and stared at my shoes. Life could hardly get better.

When we finished, we walked along the water. A steamer loomed in the harbor. I'd seen it the day before from the high piazza on Vomero, but up close it was overwhelming—a giant iron monster. We walked onto the dock. Mamma went down on one knee and smoothed my shirt across my bony chest and wiped my hands and face with the inner hem of her shawl.

From somewhere under that shawl she pulled out a little fold of cloth. It had a string tied around it. Another surprise? With her thumb, she tucked it inside my right shoe, under the arch of my foot. It was so small, it fit easily. "Your job is to survive."

"Wha—?" I opened my mouth, but she put a finger over my lips.

"First of all, simply survive." She stopped and swallowed and for a moment I thought maybe she was sick. "Watch, like you always do, watch and learn and do whatever you have to do to fit in. Talk as little as possible—just watch and use your head." Her eyes didn't blink for so long, they turned glassy. "Nothing can stop you, *tesoro mio*. Remember, you're special, a gift from the Most Powerful One. As soon as you can, get an education. Be your own boss." Then she said, "Open your mouth." I opened my mouth and she spat in it. "That's for long life." She stood up. "Don't undress with anyone around. Ever. Swear to me."

"What?"

"Swear, Beniamino."

I swallowed her saliva. "I swear, Mamma."

We held hands and walked the plank onto the ship. I looked beyond to the two mounds of Vesuvio, red in the rising sun.

A man stopped us.

"We've come to see Pier Giorgio," said Mamma.

"He went to visit his family in Calabria."

"Then we'll wait for him."

"He's not coming on this trip," said the man.

Mamma sucked in air. "That can't be." She pulled me in front of her and pressed her hands down on my shoulders so hard, I thought I'd fall. "I paid," she said. "I paid Pier Giorgio."

"For what?"

"Passage to America."

America. I reached up and put my hand on hers. That was why she had said those crazy words about survival; she was afraid of the journey. But it was worth it; we'd find our fortune in America, like Tonino. We'd send money home, enough for everyone to come and join us.

I would have whispered encouragement, but the man was arguing with her. "This is a cargo ship," he said for a second time. "No passengers."

"That can't be," said Mamma. "It's all arranged."

The man sighed. "How much have you got?"

24

"I gave it all to Pier Giorgio. My son's passage is paid."

"Go to another ship. Give him to a *padrone*—an agent—who will pay his fare in exchange for work once the ship lands."

"My son will never be anyone's slave."

"Then he's not going to America."

I looked up at Mamma to ask her what was going on. But she put a hand over my mouth and stared at the man. "Yes, he is." She took off her shawl. The cloth of her dress seemed thin and shabby, like gauze. In an instant my strong mamma changed into someone small and weak. I wanted to cover her up.

The man rubbed his dirt-caked neck, leaving a clean streak of olive flesh. Then he took us down a ladder. We stepped off at the first inside deck, but the ladder kept going down. "Go hide in the dark, boy, past those barrels and boxes. Don't make a peep till you feel the sea moving under you. Even then wait a full hour before you come up. Promise."

I looked at Mamma. She nodded. "I promise." I took Mamma's hand, to lead her to the right spot, but he slapped my hand away.

"Your mother has to hide in a different spot, for safety. Hurry up now. Go."

My eyes stung. I blinked hard. This was nothing, nothing at all, compared to being in the grotto under the convent with the body and the rats. This was simple.

I felt my way into the dark. When I looked back, Mamma and the man no longer stood in the circle of light that came in above the ladder. I went farther. Finally, I sat. But the floorboards were wet. They smelled of vinegar. So

I climbed onto a barrel lid. Other smells came at me—machine oils and salted foods and wine and olive oil. And, strangest of all, hay.

Soon men climbed up and down the ladder, disappearing below or above, mercifully not stopping on this deck.

My skin prickled, but I didn't rub my arms. My bottom went numb from not changing position, but I didn't flinch. My tongue felt fat against the roof of my mouth, but I didn't open my jaw. There were noises from the deck above as though hundreds of people were up there. And there were quiet sounds, too, now and then in the dark nearby. The labored breathing of a frightened person. Mamma. I wanted to call out to her. But I had promised not to.

After a while, scraping sounds came from the deck below, then the whoosh of fire and the roar of the steam engine. I heard a clank and all light ceased.

Only babies were afraid of the dark.

A horn blasted over and over, and I felt the movement of the sea. We were going. Going to America.

I waited in the dark. More than an hour, it had to be more. I waited in the heat that grew until I was drenched with sweat. Then I whispered, "Mamma."

CHAPTER FOUR

Whispers

"*Zitto*—quiet," came a hot hiss of sour breath. A man's voice.

I twisted my neck and peered into the dark. I couldn't see him, but someone was near. "Where's Mamma?"

"Halfway back to hell by now," came the raspy voice.

Catholics talked that way—hell this and hell that. I got off the barrel and felt my way in the direction of the ladder, calling loudly, "Mamma."

"Stop," said the man. "Come back and shut up. Someone might hear you."

Yes. "Mamma!" I pressed forward. I'd find her and we'd climb to the top deck and see America.

Something caught my pants at the hip. I pulled and the cloth came free with a small rip.

"They'll throw you overboard," said the man.

That stopped me. I swam good; I wouldn't drown, no matter how deep it was. But I didn't know which way America was. And what if they threw Mamma overboard, too? With her shawl on, she might sink.

A long time passed, enough for my shoulders to ache from holding them tight and still. Think—use my head, like Mamma said. People couldn't just throw other people overboard. Weren't there laws against things like that? And even if there weren't, someone would have to have a terrible reason to do such a terrible thing.

I slid my foot forward silently. My path was blocked. I pushed at crates. "Mamma." I whispered as loud as I dared. "Mamma, Mamma."

"Don't doubt me, boy. We're too far from port to turn around. If they find us, we'll be food for the fish. There's no other way to get rid of us."

"Why would they want to get rid of us?" I said.

"No one has pity on sick stowaways. We could infect the ship; then they wouldn't let anyone debark in America. They won't take that chance. I hear that if a sailor lets a sick guy on, they throw him overboard, too."

I wasn't sick. Neither was Mamma. We wouldn't get thrown overboard.

I had to get away from this sick man. I tried to climb over the crates. Impossible.

Mamma was nowhere near. Even if she hadn't overheard our conversation, she would have called out for me by now if she was down here. But she knew where I was. She'd come find me.

"I shouldn't be a stowaway," said the man in a tired

voice. "I paid my passage. I was supposed to go to America in steerage, on a regular ship. It took years to earn the money." He stopped talking. Too bad. At least his voice was a kind of company.

The boat pitched and made my stomach lurch.

The man groaned. "Leave it to me to pick up cholera, so they wouldn't take me, even with a ticket. But last night I heard people saying this cargo ship was heading to New York. I was practically crawling, but I snuck on."

I shook my head, though he couldn't see me in the dark. "New York? I thought we were going to America?"

"New York is America, boy. Don't you know anything? New York is paradise. The opposite of your little hovel in Napoli. The opposite of where your mamma is."

"Mamma is here. On the boat."

"No, she's not. She stuck you here so you can go to America and make a life for yourself."

"Mamma's hiding. She's on the top deck."

"Are you crazy? No hiding places up there."

"Then she's on the deck below. She's here!" I pushed hard at the crates. I threw myself against them, over and over. Finally some tumbled away, me with them. I stumbled forward till I finally grasped the ladder. It was as though I was in the grotto all over again—the panic I felt at the bottom of the ladder, the relief that came as I climbed.

At the top was a metal hatch. I heaved my back against it and it opened. Sunlight streamed in, all wonderful. The cool sea air swelled my lungs. "Mamma," I hollered. "Mamma, where are you?"

A man pulled me from the hole. "What do we have here? A talking rat?"

Talking? Mamma had said to talk as little as possible. I dangled by one arm from the man's hand, the breeze knocking me about.

"No, a silent rat," said the man who had told me where to hide. He came running over and shot me a warning glance.

I pulled myself free and gingerly walked a few steps along the deck toward a herd of cattle with pigs snorting among them. It was their hooves I must have heard before—that was what had made me think there were a hundred people on board. Beyond them was the terrifying sea in every direction. Green, swelling and falling, on and on forever.

Find Mamma. But the railing was two levels of pipes, with so much space below and between them that there was nothing to stop me from flying into the water with the next pitch of the ship. A mast rose thick and sturdy off to my left with a high pile of oily cloth folded beside it. I went toward it, my shoes slipping on the wet deck, arms reaching. I made it!

I climbed onto the pile of cloth, clung to the mast, and looked around. I saw men. Men, but no women. Not a single one.

CHAPTER FIVE

Brooms

"Come on." A hand tugged my elbow.

My arms and legs were wrapped around the mast as if I was a monkey. My bottom was on the oily cloth, getting dirty, which didn't matter, since I'd wet my pants. I had yelled for Mamma, then cried myself to sleep.

"Get up."

I hated all these men. They had seen me cry. And none of them would bring me to Mamma.

"Food," the man said, lifting his eyebrows. "Come."

Food? His face looked nice, almost kind. But I looked at the sea beyond the open deck and hugged the mast tighter.

He grabbed my shirt and pulled me down. "You'll get your sea legs soon," he said. "For now, take the middle path." And he let go.

I stood unsteady, arms to both sides. Path? All I saw were animals packed against one another and thick ropes coiled high. And pipes and rigging and barrels and life-boats and the big white funnel horn.

"Follow me." The man went straight toward the ani-mals. Just then, the ship rolled and I fell on all fours. He grabbed me by the arm and we staggered through the an-imals. The cows had to be thumped hard to get them to move. The pigs grunted and threatened to charge.

We came to a second mast and a set of steps up to a raised area near the prow of the ship. A circle of men sat there, stripped to the waist. They made space for us.

Fresh bread passed from hand to hand. Then came dripping mozzarella, so new my fingers left dents.

"This'll be the last mozzarella till America," said a man.

I caught the white drops of its milk in my hunk of bread. Slices of salami came around, wet to the touch. I didn't take any; they were made from pig. But I let myself smell my fingers after I'd passed it on: spicy and lemony. Then came tomatoes.

If the men had prayed before they ate, I hadn't seen it. And no one covered his head. They didn't act like my family—they didn't talk about how good the meal was and how thankful they were, even though this food was plenti-ful and delicious.

"Where's Mamma? She's hungry, too."

"Your mother again?" said a man. "Eat, and we'll worry about her later."

Nonna's proverb came to me: *"Chi tene mamma, nun chiagne"*—Whoever has a mother doesn't cry. I held my breath to stop the tears, but they came anyway.

The men jabbered on, not looking at me. I should have been grateful, but their ignoring me only made me feel more alone. They talked about the trip: two weeks if we were lucky and didn't hit storms. It could be three weeks. Four.

All that time at sea. How far was America, anyway?

They passed around a bottle of wine, each one taking a swill. When it came to me, I hesitated.

"What's the matter, aren't you weaned yet? You want milk?" asked a man jokingly.

They laughed.

I tried it. It was strong—not like the sweet wine we had at Passover. I didn't like it, but I was thirsty. I drank again, then passed the bottle.

But now they were all looking at me and talking about me, as though they'd suddenly been reminded I was there. The man who had brought me over from the mast said, "I'm Carlo. You get an extra tomato since you didn't eat the salami."

"I'll save it for Mamma."

"Don't worry about your mother," said the man who had spoken before. "Just eat."

"Why should he eat more?" said a man gruffly. "He's another mouth to feed—a useless mouth."

Still, Carlo handed me a tomato so ripe and sweet, its juices burst in my mouth. I finished it and wiped my chin with my palm, then licked my hand.

"At least he appreciates a tomato," said one man. And the others laughed again.

They went around the circle introducing themselves. Then they asked my name. Beniamino was a typical Jewish name. These men weren't Jewish—not the way they'd devoured that salami. I remembered Mamma taking my yarmulke off. I shrugged.

"A talking rat with no name," said Eduardo, the one who had lifted me from the top of the ladder. A cigarette bobbled between his lips as he spoke.

"He must have slipped in last night early," said Carlo, "because we had someone guarding the plank from midnight on."

I glanced at Franco, the man who had snuck Mamma and me onto the boat this morning. He was looking at me, his face tense.

". . . quieter than a rat," Carlo was saying. "More like a mouse in church. What shall we call the mouse we see at Mass on *domenica*—on Sunday?" He clapped. "Let's call him Domenico."

"In America, though, he'll need an American name," said Eduardo. "Joe would be better."

"Or just make Domenico short—Dom—like the Americans do," said Carlo. "After all, he's a little fellow."

They laughed. Most of them had lit cigarettes by now, and they were blowing their smoke into the breeze.

"What'll it be, little mouse?" asked Eduardo. "Joe or Dom?"

"Dom," I said.

"See?" said Eduardo to Franco. "A talking mouse."

"What do they call you in America?" I asked Eduardo.

"I don't need an American name," he said. "I'm not staying when we land. You'll go off to Mulberry Street. But us . . ." He looked around at the circle of men. "We go back to Napoli—*bella* Napoli. So, little mouse, little Dom, let's talk." He leaned away from me as if to get a look at my whole self, while he picked salami from between his teeth. "Is your mother really hidden on this ship?"

I stole a glance at Franco. He closed his eyes briefly. But he didn't have to, because I'd figured it out. He'd get in trouble if I told; he'd brought two more mouths to feed onto this boat.

I looked down at my hands. As soon as these men went about their business again, I'd find Mamma. On my own. And I'd bring her food. Franco would give me food for her.

"If there's a woman on board," said Carlo, "I'll be mighty happy."

The men chuckled.

"If there were other stowaways, we'd know by now," said Franco.

I remembered the sick man. "There is someone else," I blurted.

"What! Who?"

"I don't know. He talked to me, but he didn't tell me his name."

"Where is he?" asked Eduardo.

"One deck down. He was hiding in the dark near me."

Eduardo got up.

"Wait." I grabbed his ankle. "Be careful. He's sick."

Eduardo's cheek twitched. "Sick how?"

"Cholera."

He jerked free from me.

"I don't have cholera," I said. "I swear."

"Did he vomit?"

"Yes."

Eduardo's mouth twisted into a grimace. "Then he's dying."

And now they were all arguing. Everyone had heard of a different way to deal with cholera. The only thing they could agree on was that someone had to find the man. And soon.

No one volunteered.

They played a game—guessing the number of pigs on deck. The loser, a big man called Beppe, touched his forehead, his chest, his left shoulder, then his right. Aha: the sign of the cross. Catholics did that a lot. Beppe held up the medal that hung around his neck and said, "Help me, Sant'Antonio." He kissed it and disappeared down the hatch.

He came back up, holding an oil lamp. "He's breathing. But he's too far gone to answer."

One man got an oilclotch. Another got three brooms and handed them out. Beppe went back down the ladder with the lamp, leading the way to the sick man.

"Get up," said Beppe.

No response. He must have been playing dead, hoping they'd go away.

"They won't hurt you," I said. "They'll feed you. They fed me."

He didn't answer.

Two men spread the oilcloth beside him and stood holding tight the top and bottom ends. Three other men used the brooms to push him onto the cloth.

He groaned and his head lolled to one side. The black bristles of his new beard were streaked with yellow and red. "Water," he breathed roughly.

They carried him up onto the deck near the railing. Then two men lowered buckets over the side and filled them with water.

"Don't swallow," said Beppe. "It's seawater. To clean you up." And he doused the sick man with bucket after bucket.

The man's chest rose and fell. His face was clean now, and his black beard glistened.

"I've got fresh water for you," Beppe said. "Open your mouth wide."

The man opened his mouth but kept his eyes closed.

Beppe poured water into his mouth.

The sick man gulped and opened his mouth again.

Beppe poured a little more.

The sick man lay there with his mouth open. He didn't swallow this time. His chest stopped moving.

Someone nudged him with a broom. "He's gone."

What? He was right there. The man nudged him harder. "He's not gone," I said. "He can't be." I went closer.

Eduardo caught me by the pants and pulled me to him.

They argued about whether they should search the man's pockets for identification, since his family would want to know. But no one was ready to touch him.

They all made the sign of the cross. Then the men with brooms came forward and the rest stepped back. I knew what they were going to do before they did it. I didn't scream.

He was gone, oilcloth and all.

He was there, and then he wasn't.

They swabbed the deck. Some went down the ladder with buckets and mops to swab below, too.

I stood and watched, my legs splayed so I wouldn't fall. The spot where the man had sunk, the man who was now food for the fish, was far behind us, covered by the turbulence of our wake. He was dead when they threw him over. He was dead, he was dead, he was dead. They would never throw over a living person. They would never throw over Mamma or me.

"Your pants could use some cleaning, too, Dom," said a voice.

It took a moment before I realized the voice was talking to me. I was Dom. I looked up at Franco, who held a bucket.

"Take your pants off and dip them in here."

Never undress with anyone else around—Mamma had made me swear. And now I knew why; she had said it for the same reason she had taken my yarmulke. She didn't want people to see my circumcision and know I was Jewish. I shook my head.

"You smell, boy."

"I don't care."

"But we do." Franco wrinkled his nose. "Take off your shoes."

Why? My shoes were way too small for these men. "No."

"Suit yourself," he said. "Do you like the water?"

"I swim," I said. Then I tensed up. What did he mean?

"Oop la." And he sloshed the whole bucket right at my middle with a smile.

I stood dripping, my new shoes soaked. Before I could think straight, I raised the back of my forearm to him, fist curled tight, in the angry gesture every Napoletano recognized.

CHAPTER SIX

The Plan

I sat on the deck cleaning squid for Riccardo, the cook. I didn't like squid—they weren't kosher. The first time I cleaned them, I had to fight off revulsion. But cleaning squid took all my attention, and that was good because then I couldn't think about Mamma.

For two days I searched the whole boat for her, over and over. When I didn't find her and Franco wouldn't answer my questions, I imagined he had her in a cage off the boiler rooms. So I told Carlo. If anyone could stand up to Franco, it was Carlo. He helped me search. Everywhere.

She wasn't here.

I was alone on this ship. I hugged myself hard and pressed my back into the wall and listened to the buzz in my head. I was dizzy the rest of that day. Dizzy and nauseated.

Franco had left Mamma in Napoli. That coward. I hated him. Poor Mamma. My poor, poor mamma, frantic with worry for me.

But I had a plan. When we got to America, I wouldn't get off the cargo ship. I'd turn right around and go back to Mamma. In my prayers, I asked the Most Powerful One to tell her that, so she wouldn't cry too much. In the meantime, my job was to fit in. The first time I went into the galley and asked what I could do to help, Riccardo ignored me. So I watched. Then I shelled peas. When he saw how quick I was, he gave me all sorts of tasks.

There were tons of jobs on this ship. I looked around and did whatever needed doing. I was living Uncle Aurelio's lecture—I'd been smacked with adversity, and I'd picked myself up like any good Jew.

I swept out the poultry coops on the top deck and gathered eggs. I got my share of pecks on my hands and arms and even on the back of my neck. Fabrizio taught me how to milk the cows. And I cleaned the cabins, the galley, the bakery, the wheels and pipes and tools and water-distilling machine. I loved cleaning that machine, with the shiny compasses, wheels, and complicated gauges in the helm. I washed dishes, swept rat droppings, scrubbed the toilets. I brought the coal trimmers water while they shoveled, and raced up the ladders to the top deck to dip the rags for wiping their foreheads into the bucket of cold seawater.

The crew came to count on me. It was part of my plan. If they needed me, they'd take me back with them gladly. I couldn't tell them my plan, because stowaways were illegal. But when they discovered me on the ship on the way back, they'd be glad.

Eduardo said I reminded him of his son. He woke me in the morning and asked if I needed anything at night. And Carlo liked me, too. He made sure I got my fair share of food.

Each afternoon, when most of the crew took a nap, I sat in a corner far from everyone and practiced my private ritual. I untied the string around the tiny bundle Mamma had tucked in my right shoe and unfolded the cloth. Inside were four tassels, each made of eight strands of yarn, seven white and one blue, tied into many knots. The first time I opened the bundle, I recognized them instantly. They were holy tassels—*tzitzit*—from my grandfather's prayer shawl. I held them and let memories wash me clean.

My grandfather Nonno had had a beautiful prayer shawl—a *tallit*. My uncles had beautiful ones, too. But theirs were combinations of blues and greens and yellows. Nonno's was a mix of extravagantly bright swatches of red silk fabrics stitched together with fine embroidery. And it was so long that even with his arms hanging by his sides, it draped down a full hand's length past his fingertips.

From the four corners of that shawl hung these tassels. In synagogue, I used to stand beside Nonno and hold a tassel and count the knots. When we got home and he took it off, he let me help him fold it. I smoothed the tassels and wondered what secret message the Hebrew letters across the top of the *tallit* held.

Nonno died when I was five. We buried him in his *tallit*. But Nonna saved the tassels. When I turned thirteen, I'd get my own prayer shawl at my Bar Mitzvah, with these tassels at the corners.

Mamma had put them in my shoe for safekeeping.

I fingered the knots. Then I rubbed my shoes with that small piece of cloth. Not because they were dirty. No, no. They were perfectly clean. I didn't wear them; they were too slippery to walk around the ship in. And it would have been impossible to keep them dry. So I stored them in a bale of hay. I rubbed them every day—at first to make them soft again, because they'd dried hard after Franco had thrown the water on me, but later just as part of my ritual.

While I worked, I thought of Mamma. Mamma, who had wanted a better life—the life of people who wore shoes even when they were children. We'd have been together on the trip to that better life in America if it wasn't for Franco.

When I got back home, I'd go to school. Then in a few years I'd have my Bar Mitzvah and Nonna could attach these tassels to my prayer shawl and I'd get a good job. The first thing I'd do with my money was buy us ship tickets. We would live Mamma's dream, that better life.

In the meantime, being on this boat wasn't so bad. Sometimes I'd stand at the rail, holding tight, and look out at sea, pretending to be a pirate scouting for ships to raid. There were lots of dolphins, and Riccardo taught me how to spot whales. Sometimes, when we threw garbage over the side, sharks came close enough to the surface to give me goose bumps.

I finished cleaning the squid now and carried the bowls to the galley. Even when the sea was rough, I kept my footing. All it had taken was one storm to teach me perfect balance.

The crew usually ate out on the poop deck, where I'd

had my first meal with them. This was the best part of the day; the men talked till the stars came out. I headed there now. The men were already sitting around.

"Maybe I'll stay this time," said Franco. "Maybe I'll join the line on Ellis Island and make my fortune in New York."

"You can have it," said Ivo. "They speak too much gobbledy-gook there. English, bah."

"English?" said Franco. "They don't speak English in America. They speak English in England."

"Shows how much you know. In New York they speak English and German."

"And Irish," said Carlo.

"What are you all, idiots?" said Ivo. "Most Irish people speak English. Just in a funny way. Like the people from Avellino speak Napoletano funny. Nah," he said. "You can have New York. You go ahead, sound like a dumb immigrant your whole life, with everyone laughing at you. I've heard the ship officers talk about it. People even laugh at them when they go into town. For me, if I was going to jump ship, why, I'd go to South America any day. They speak Spanish there. It's like Napoletano, I hear. It's easy."

"Or Africa," said Salvatore. "In Tripoli, they respect Italians so much, they learn Italian rather than making the Italians learn African. That's where I'd go."

All this talk of different languages was news to me. I'd thought everyone everywhere spoke pretty much the same, except that Jews spoke Hebrew in synagogue, Catholics spoke Latin in church, and Muslims spoke Arabic in the mosque. Maybe when I got rich, I'd take Mamma to

South America instead of New York. If English sounded awful, who needed it?

That night as I lay in my usual spot on the floor under Eduardo's bunk, he leaned over. "Hey, Dom? You awake?"

"Sure," I said.

"Tomorrow, when we land . . ."

"We land tomorrow? Already?"

"Already? We're ten days overdue because of those storms. Anyway, when we land, you have to stay out of sight in the bunk room till I tell you. I'll find a way for you to sneak off. But you have to be quick about it. The captain said we're leaving the same day we arrive because we're so far behind schedule. So you have to do what I say when I say it. Understand?"

"Yes."

"Do you have people waiting for you in New York?"

"No."

"That's what I was afraid of." He gave a brief whistle. "There are plenty of kids on their own in America, but it's hard. Harder than in Napoli. Head for Mulberry Street."

"Why?"

"That's where Napoletani live. You'll understand them, know what's going on. I have a cousin there, but he's a son of a gun. Otherwise I'd tell you to look him up."

"Okay," I said, "Mulberry Street." What did it matter? I wasn't going anywhere but home to *bella* Napoli.

"Stay how you are, Dom, exactly how you are—make yourself useful. You know how to do it. But don't trust anyone."

"Except Napoletani," I said, "Napoletani on Mulberry Street."

"Especially don't trust them. Napoletani cheat everyone. Remember that."

"But you don't have to cheat in America," I said. "Everyone's rich."

"What a sack of lies. My cousin, jerk that he is, told me the truth. It's tough all over, especially at the bottom, where you'll be. Take care of yourself, Dom, because no one else will."

I didn't answer.

"In bocca al lupo," he said—In the mouth of the wolf. It was a roundabout way of wishing me luck without challenging fate.

"Crepi," I answered—May it burst and die—the standard response.

"And don't forget your shoes," said Eduardo. He pulled his head back up.

Snores came from many bunks.

I rolled on my side. We would be in America the next day.

A match struck, and the little flame lit the cigarette between Franco's lips. His face appeared old, all the crags deep in shadow. Smoking wasn't allowed anywhere except on the open deck. But there was no one awake to notice. No one but me.

"Go put your shoes on," said Franco.

"What?"

"Eduardo's right. You're sleeping with them on tonight. So you'll be ready in the morning."

I put on my shoes, careful to place the cloth with the tassels under my right arch, and crawled back beneath Eduardo's bunk.

Eventually, Franco's cigarette went out. Then the smell

of the smoke faded. There was nothing but the quiet noises of sleepers and the background rumble of the boiler and engines.

I stared into the dark.

The funnel horn woke me. I was groggy from too little sleep, but I jumped up. I raced to the open deck to find everyone else working even though it was barely morning. We were pulling into a gigantic harbor. People and horses and wagons jammed the shore. Another cargo ship unloaded sheep in clumps of three, lifting them with pulleys from the deck, swinging them over the railing, and plopping them onto the dock. Bells clanged, horns blew, the air shook with bleats and shouts.

Someone smacked the back of my head.

"Get to the bunk room till it's time," said Eduardo. "You'll only make trouble for everyone if they see you now."

So I ran, but not to the bunks. I hid in the dairy cow house. I strained to see between the slats, but I couldn't make out much. The noise went on for hours.

I had slept through breakfast, so I patted my favorite cow and squirted hot milk into my mouth.

The heat of the cows and the milk in my belly and the roar of the world outside . . . I'd gone to bed so late . . . I dozed off.

When I woke, I peeked between the slats. The men were already loading things for the return trip. Lined up nearby were crates marked with the post office symbol. I'd always wanted to get a letter—and to write one. I knew exactly what went into a letter, because I listened when Uncle Vittorio read the mail for women in our neighborhood. Many of the men didn't read, either. Mamma could have read for them, but no one asked her to. The women said Mamma was uppity to know how to read like that.

Mamma Mamma Mamma. I pressed the heels of my hands against my eyelids to stop the tears. This was a trick the journey had taught me. Sometimes I sat for hours with the heels of my hands against my eyelids.

Then the horn blared and the plank was drawn up and the ship pulled away from the dock. I was going home. I whooped for joy.

The door of the cow house opened. "It's you!" Franco's shocked face was in mine. "You idiot! We're leaving already."

"I'm going back to Napoli."

"A promise is a promise." Franco dragged me out. "You said you knew how to swim. So swim." And he threw me overboard.

CHAPTER SEVEN

Waiting

The water was farther down than I'd thought. Far enough for me to scream, far enough for me to think I was dead. I hit it with a smack and went under so deep, I couldn't see anything.

I put my hands over my head and swam upward as fast as I could. My hands split the water and slammed down to push me up, up. I gasped to fill my burning lungs.

The swirl of water from the screw-propeller engine of my own ship pulled me under. I swam away with all my might, broke the surface, gasped, got sucked under all over again.

But then my ship was gone, and I was alone in the water. With another ship coming in to harbor.

I swam for the dock and latched on to a piling

pole. Barnacles cut my hands and arms. I shouted. I imagined the huge ship crushing me against the pole as I screamed for help.

The ship made the water rise and fall and swirl. It splashed over my head and pulled me. If I let go and swam under the dock, I might get sucked down again and not have the strength to swim up this time. So I held on with my whole body, despite the barnacles, curling myself as tight as I could, praying that none of me stuck out past the dock's edge.

The bang of the ship against the dock sent a shudder through my pole, but the ship didn't touch me.

I was cold. Bleeding. Exhausted.

And alive.

Shouts of joy came from the ship as people walked down the plank.

I called out. The people were looking around in wonder at the new world in front of them; surely someone would glance down between the ship and the dock. Just one person, that was all I needed. That man in the suit, or that woman in the fancy dress. I kept calling. My throat grew hoarse. But who could hear me?

Soon the passengers were gone and the crew unloaded luggage. No one was looking around in wonder anymore.

I cried out again. My neck hurt from straining. I let my head fall.

After a long while, a holler came from above. I looked up. A man on the dock jabbered at me frantically.

"Help," I tried to shout, but it came out as a croak.

"Italian?" he screeched.

A man with a large mustache appeared and looked down at me. "What are you doing there?" His words sounded strange—but I understood.

"I fell."

"Can you swim?"

"Yes."

"Swim under the dock. I'll throw you a rope on the other side." He disappeared.

The first man still jabbered at me.

I didn't move.

Eventually the Italian man came back. "Go. Go to the other side. It's not safe to pull you up on the side with the ship. Understand?"

"I'll wait," I said.

"For what?"

"Till the ship leaves."

"Only first and second class were allowed to disembark. The rest of the passengers won't be processed for days."

I had no idea what that meant.

"Did you hear me? The ship won't leave for three days, at the least."

I whimpered.

"Stay put. I'll find someone who can swim." His face disappeared again.

In a little while gasping breaths came from under the dock.

"Here," I called out. "I'm here."

An older man swam to me. He grabbed the pole, then cursed as he pulled his bleeding hand away. He carried the end of a rope between his teeth. He took it out and offered it to me.

I didn't let go of the pole. I couldn't. I was stuck.

The man grabbed my ear and twisted.

"Aiii!" I let go of the pole with one hand and clawed at him.

He looped the rope around my chest and gave a yank, and I was jerked away through the water. I spun; water went up my nose and down my throat. I was drowning. Then I was suddenly out in the air, swinging like a clump of seaweed on a hook. I landed in a heap on the hot dock.

Someone asked me in plain language who I was, but my eyes were closed against the bright sun and I wasn't sure I could open them. My bones ached from being in the cold water; my teeth chattered.

I could hear men talking, trying to guess how I'd gotten down there, who I was. That had to be my passenger ship—it was from Napoli, and my speech told them I was, too. And I had to be a boy from a good family with shoes like that. I must have fallen off the plank when the first- and second-class passengers disembarked. Someone would surely pay a reward for their saving me. They argued about who deserved the reward. Then they worried that instead of a reward, they'd get blamed for my winding up in the water. That ended that.

Someone wrapped a padded crate cloth around me and rubbed my back and arms and legs through the cloth. Gradually, warmth radiated from my middle. But I still wouldn't open my eyes. I wanted whoever was holding me to keep holding me.

He carried me, bumping through crowds. I took a peek. Everyone was rushing. They talked funny. And they carried canes and wore so many clothes—jackets and hats.

Even the men working the docks had on shirts under that beating sun.

He carried me into a brick building filled with people in nice clothes, packed together. Men in uniforms stood beside them, holding on to giant handcarts of baggage. He spoke to a man who called out strange things through his megaphone. Another man came running and took the megaphone and announced in plain language, "Who's missing a Napoletano boy?" He pointed at me.

"What a nightmare for his parents," a woman said. "Take him back to the ship right away."

A man touched the rip in my pants, the one I'd gotten my first day on the ship. It had grown so big, I could put my hand through it. "You're third class." He wagged his head. Another man pulled me by the hand back to the dock and up onto the ship and left me there.

What? Just like that?

The crew was still unloading luggage, and no one seemed to have noticed me. I scrambled over by a mast, out of the way, and watched. The heat of the day slowly dried me. The drier I got, the better I felt. Life was looking up; I was back on a ship. A passenger ship. This might even be better than my cargo ship.

I wandered into a room with a bed and desk and many ledgers. One lay open, listing name after name. This was the record of passengers. I had to stay out of the way of whoever kept it.

I walked out quickly, my heart thumping, and went straight to a group of lifeboats along the side. I held on to the rail and looked down and tried to blend with the background.

Time passed, and no one came to chase me away.

The smell of food got me wandering again. I hadn't eaten since that squirt of cow's milk. A crew member glanced at me, then stopped his work to look again. I ran to the closest hatch and scooted down below deck.

I sank into a sea of people. Most were quiet, putting their energy into the struggle to breathe in this heat. Some grumbled that they weren't allowed up on deck. The only people left on the ship now were third-class passengers. A man said there were five hundred and twenty of them, all in a stench of vomit and feces.

Here in the dark, no one could see beyond arm's length. But there was bread with lard spread, salty and delicious. And all I really needed to do was stay on this ship.

Home to Mamma. It was just a matter of time. My mamma.

The officers allowed us to sleep on the top deck. Babies cried, men cursed.

I was too wound up to do anything but wander among them. I found a man and two boys wearing yarmulkes, but I couldn't understand them. So I hung around Napoletani and listened. They pointed at a statue in the harbor and fell to their knees in prayer. I thought often of Uncle Aurelio and his speeches about *le possibilità*.

The next day the quarantine station officers came on board. People had been warning one another about them. They checked for typhus, yellow fever, smallpox. The trick was to stand at attention, look alert, and, no matter what, not cough. I was grateful to know the trick. Some who didn't were taken off someplace. It was rumored that they went into observation far away, and if they got sicker, they went into isolation somewhere even farther away. After that, who knew what became of them?

That second night, I took my shoes off and spread out my socks to air. I carefully tucked the cloth with the tassels inside one sock, and I used, instead, the corner of the padded crate cloth that I carried everywhere to rub the shoe leather soft, because it had dried hard again after being in the water. When I went to put my shoes back on, I couldn't find my socks.

My *tzitzit*—my tassels!

No!

I felt all over the floor around me. I ran through the clusters of people, looking everywhere. I tugged on women's skirts and asked for help. I looked and looked and looked.

No no no.

My grandfather's prayer shawl tassels were gone. America had thieves, like Napoli—but worse ones. Far worse.

I stared out over the buildings of New York and pressed the heels of my hands against my eyelids. Still the tears came. I brushed them away as fast as they fell.

Some of those buildings seemed as tall as Vesuvio. But they didn't make me feel uplifted, like the high building of my synagogue in Napoli. Instead, I felt tiny and weak.

I turned my back to them and looked at the statue the others had prayed to—the grand Statue of Liberty.

I didn't want liberty. I stood there snuffling. All I wanted was to go home.

CHAPTER EIGHT

On Land

When it was time to disembark, men put gold chains around their necks, then ties and vests and coats, and they combed their mustaches. Women pinned their hair and put on jackets and fancy shoes with big wooden heels and any number of rings. Even the children sprouted boots and coats. I was a *scugnizzo* compared to them. And I was the only one missing a label—they all had a big number three pinned to their jackets, for third class. I tucked my shirt in my pants and smoothed the front of it.

The men carried baggage in both hands. So did the women, unless they were carrying a child or two. Some had an infant strapped to their chest. Everyone clenched their health certificate in their teeth.

I held my padded cloth and tried to blend in. I had a plan. As we filed along, I was going to duck into the cow house. It had worked last time—almost. All I needed was to stay on this ship until it left for home.

But when I opened the cow house door, the woman behind me shouted, and a man from Napoli pulled me back into the crowd. He said, "What? You want to go to England? America is better." Stupid me, to think that because this ship had left from the port of Napoli, it would return there.

Now I needed another plan.

The crowd carried me along, deafened by boat horns blasting from every direction, down the plank, around crates and animals and wagons on the pier, into the customs building. When it was my turn, the officer simply waved me past, and again the crowd carried me, this time onto a barge, men going to one side, and women and children to the other. They piled the baggage between us.

In less than half an hour we were ferried across to Ellis Island, and our shipload of passengers merged with shiploads from all over the world. No one understood anyone else. We went into a giant building. I'd never seen a building with wood walls. In Napoli only shacks were made of wood, not homes, and certainly not official buildings. On the bottom floor was a baggage area. Everyone was told to place their belongings there, but no one wanted to. The official kept saying that they could fetch them after they'd passed through the registration room upstairs. Still, no one put anything down.

The official lost patience; he barked at us.

Everyone's eyes darted around. Then they opened their bundles and layered extra clothes onto already sweating bodies. Around their necks they hung picture lockets and saint medals and keys to the homes they'd left behind. They loaded their pockets with bone fans and wood pipes and rolling pins and little bottles and all kinds of documents. A woman from Napoli took out needle and thread and sewed letters from her dead husband into the hem of her skirt. She said they were love letters. Some people locked their fingers around the handles of their suitcases and simply refused to give them up.

Mamma's voice called, *"Tesoro? Tesoro mio?"*

I whirled around and watched a boy run to the fat, short woman who had stolen Mamma's voice, stolen Mamma's name for me—treasure. She said, "Grab hold of my skirt and don't let go, no matter what."

That was what Mamma would say to me. My heart raced. I had to bite my hand to keep from screaming.

I threw my padded crate cloth onto the baggage pile and joined the crowd on the stairs. Everyone was talking and telling everyone else to hush so they could figure out what was going on. I stayed close to Napoletani. If they understood anything and repeated it, I would understand, too.

At the top of the stairs doctors checked fingernails and the backs of legs. They opened collars and felt necks. Women shuddered, their faces tight with fear, for they'd never been touched like that before. The doctors made everyone take off hats and kerchiefs, and they parted hair to inspect scalps. Men with pompadours were yelled at, as though they were trying to hide something in their puffed-up hair. Then the doctors took out metal hooks—like the kind people used to button their shoes—and looked inside lower eyelids. All that took only seconds.

Children screamed constantly. Doctors wanted to make sure any child over two years old was healthy enough to walk alone, but the children clung to their mothers. So the doctors ripped them away and walked off several paces with them, then set them down to go shrieking back.

I watched everything closely. Watch and learn and fit in—that was what Mamma said.

Almost everyone was pushed on into the giant registration room. But now and then the doctors made a mark with colored chalk on a person's clothes. The mark was always a letter; I saw *S, B, X, C, H, L, E, K, F, G, N.* Sometimes there were two letters, *Ft, Pg, CT, Sc,* or sometimes an *X* inside a circle. All the letters meant something bad, because they were written on people a doctor had spent extra time with. A man took off his coat and turned it inside out to hide the mark on his lapel.

The doctor who inspected me took five seconds. He touched the scabs on my arms from the barnacles on the piling pole at the dock and said something to me in English. I stood at attention, without coughing—I remembered the trick. Then he said something to the woman behind me and she shrugged. Two women in white uniforms—nurses— came up. One pulled me to the side. She did things with her hands, sticking up one finger, then five, then three, or forming an O with her thumb and index finger. The other woman mimicked her. Then the nurse turned to me and made a shape with her hand. She waited. I looked at her. The other nurse mimicked the shape. They both looked at me. And I got it; I made the shape. The first nurse took me through several shapes. Then she drew shapes on a piece of paper and I had to copy them. She smiled at me and patted me on the back and pointed for me to go join the lines in the registration room.

I'd passed another test. Though what it meant was beyond me. I got in line and looked back at the nurses. They were still watching me, with suspicious eyes now. So I moved ahead through the line, out of their sight, till I found two men speaking Napoletano. I stood behind them and looked up at their faces as though I knew them. After a while I snuck a glance back; the nurses were testing someone else. I heard a man say they were testing for idiocy. So they'd thought I was an idiot.

This was the first time in my life I'd ever stood in a real line. Napoletani waited for things in clusters. But here, there were three strict lines. I was in the one on the left. I couldn't see the front, so I kept my ears open and I looked out the side windows at the Statue of Liberty. She was green in this light, and her torch was bright gold. A barge pulled in with more people. Where would they all fit? I looked at the floor. It was tiled, like any floor in Napoli. But it was dirty. Why was everyone coming to a place where people worked in wood buildings with dirty floors?

The lines moved slowly, but finally I could see an inspector at the head of each one. The inspector for my line questioned everyone in English. When they answered in another language, he called over a man in uniform who could speak every language in the world. The men in front of me called him a translator. Everyone handed over documents and pulled money out of pockets and hems of coats. The inspector asked questions and handed it all back, including the money.

A woman in the next line cried to her husband. She

wasn't from Napoli, but I could understand her. Their child had gotten a chalk mark on his jacket because he was sick. The nurses said they'd have to take him away. She was afraid to let him go. At the same time she was afraid that if she didn't, they'd all be sent back. I wanted to tell her they'd be lucky if they were sent back. As soon as I reached that inspector, I would tell him everything and be sent home.

The two Napoletani in front of me practiced what they were going to say.

One of them played the inspector: "Do you have a job?"

The other answered, "Yes, at . . ."

"No!" said the first one. "It's illegal to have a *padrone* who got you a job ahead of time. You say, 'No.' "

"But we paid all that money. We have a *padrone*, right?"

"Of course we do. He's waiting for us when we get out. Okay, second question. Where are you going to live?"

"I don't know."

"No! You say, 'At my cousin's on Mulberry Street.' With as little money as we have, unless we say we have a place to stay, they'll send us to the Board of Inquiry, who will send us back to Napoli. Listen, you be the inspector. Ask me what I'll do in America."

"What will you do in America?"

"Anything. I will take any job I am offered. See? That's the right answer. Ask me about money."

"What about money?"

"We have to have enough. That's what I just said. Show the inspector all your money." He sighed. "They have to let us stay—we can't go back to starving. Look, I'll answer first.

Listen and you say the same thing when it's your turn. Understand?"

"I understand."

I doubted the second man understood anything. But I understood. And I was happy. I had no money. They'd send me home for sure.

Finally, the inspector talked to the two men. The translator spoke our language pretty good. The inspector checked their names against the ship's list. He asked if they could read, if they were sick, if they were married, if they'd committed crimes, what their occupations were, if they were anarchists—on and on, ending with how much money they had. The men couldn't write, so the translator wrote answers for them.

I glanced over at the next line. The inspector there asked a woman if she was married. He asked her that shameless question with her child holding her hand, right in front of her husband. She stiffened at the insult and her husband objected in a fierce voice.

Mamma had to put up with insults because of me all the time. And it dawned on me: right now, wherever she was, she didn't have to. Anyone new who met her didn't have to know she had a child. They could ask, "Do you have a child at home?" and she could answer, "No." She could get an office job—the right kind of job for someone who could read. Maybe she had one already.

That would be good. If she had a job, she couldn't cry all day about missing me. And when I got back, she could keep the job, because her boss would realize by then how smart and useful she was. Life would be better.

The man behind me pushed me forward. The inspector spoke to me in loud English. It was clear he was annoyed. He must have been talking to me while I was thinking about Mamma.

"I want to go to Napoli," I said.

"Ah," said the translator, "another from Napoli. Where are your parents?"

"Everyone I know is in Napoli."

"No no, I'm talking about here. Where are your parents in this room?"

"I'm alone. I want to go to Napoli. I have no money."

The man lowered his head toward me. "What's your name?"

Should I tell the truth? Beniamino, the name I was born with, or Dom, the name the cargo crew had given me?

"You know your name, boy. What is it?"

I shook my head.

"A lost child," said the translator.

"There are lots of lost children," said another translator. He stood in front of the middle line, and the way he talked, I knew he'd grown up in Napoli. "Put him out on the front steps. His agent—some tricky *padrone*—will find him."

"I don't think he has one. He must have come on that big ship—the *Città di Napoli*. That ship's careful not to break the law; they don't let on children who belong to a *padrone*. He must have lost his family."

"Then his father's in this crowd," said the Napoletano translator. "Don't worry. The father will find him."

"He'll stay with you, then, Giosè."

"I'm as busy as you are. I can't worry about a little

scugnizzo." The Napoletano translator turned away and spoke to the people at the front of that line.

"My inspector says you have to keep him beside you till his father shows up," my translator said, then gestured to the man behind me to come forward.

"I'm not babysitting him," said Giosè.

"Look," said my translator. He pointed at my shoes. "This is no urchin. The father will be grateful. Maybe I should keep him myself to get the reward."

Giosè blinked at my shoes. I might not have had socks, but my shoes looked beautiful. "What am I supposed to do with you? All right, you've got shoes. You're somebody's little *signore*. Get over here and stand behind me."

I stood behind Giosè. My arms hung at my sides like dead fish. It was too hard to keep fighting. Soon enough they'd realize I had no father here and they'd have to send me home.

The lines went on forever. Giosè told me that more than five thousand people would pass through these lines that day. I knew that was huge.

The immigrants were almost all men, some in their teens. They talked about how wonderful they knew America was and how they would send for their wives and mothers and sisters soon, as though Giosè would be impressed and treat them better. But he didn't really look at them, and he did a lot of sighing. Many of the men held books and read to one another.

When Giosè went to the bathroom, I asked the man at the front of the line, "What are the stories about?"

He smiled proudly. "These are no stories. This book is

teaching me how to speak English. Listen." He spouted off gobbledy-gook. Then he waited.

It took a second before I knew what he wanted; I clapped.

He pressed his palm against his chest. "I'm a skilled artisan and now I speak English. I'm going to get a good job making beautiful furniture." His breath was foul, and I found myself staring at a tiny black bug jumping in his hair. I stepped away.

Giosè came back and the morning went by slowly. Every time I sank to a squat, he told me to stand again so my father could find me.

My father.

Mamma hadn't ever told anyone who my father was.

I imagined him now. He'd have black eyes. His nose would be straight—because mine was straight and Mamma's was crooked, so I must have gotten my nose from him. He'd be able to read. Mamma never would have chosen an uneducated man.

Maybe Giosè was right; maybe my father was here. I stared at each man. None of them looked at me.

After a while I switched to staring at the boys. They came in groups, ranging from six years old up, and most of them were with an uncle.

Giosè whispered, "Those men aren't really uncles. They're hired by the *padroni* to bring the boys over. A *padrone* pays a man's ticket. In return, the man watches over the boys until they get through immigration. Then the 'uncle' goes on his way." Giosè brushed off his hands. "And the boys begin work for the *padrone*. It's illegal, but that doesn't stop anyone."

The boys were barefoot, skinny, and dirty. Their "uncle" barked orders, and they obeyed immediately.

I stared at one boy. Mucus crusted his cheek and there was a colored chalk mark on his shirt. His "uncle" pointed at me. "That one, he's my nephew, too."

Giosè shook his head as though he'd been right all along about me. "Get over there behind your uncle."

"I don't know him," I yelped. "I've never seen him before."

The "uncle" grabbed me by the elbow and flung me behind him.

CHAPTER NINE

Trust

"No!" I screamed. "I don't know him!"

"Shut up," said the "uncle."

"Send me back to Napoli!" I screamed.

The "uncle" smacked me across the jaw with the back of his hand. I fell. He went on answering Giosè's questions.

The other boys turned their backs to us, but one of them hissed out of the side of his mouth. "Stupid. You'll have work in America. And food. Get up."

I wouldn't get up. I'd done what Mamma said. I'd watched and learned and fit in. And none of it mattered, because now this "uncle" had me and I'd be lost and alone for the rest of my life. I lay there and screamed.

The "uncle" kicked me. "Get up, or they'll throw

you in a home with sick boys and you'll die." He turned back to Giosè.

My side hurt. I drew my knees to my chest and hugged them.

"That's where I'm going," said the boy with the colored chalk mark on his shirt, "to the sick home. To die." His eyes were glassy with fever.

"I'm going to Napoli!" I forced out as loud as I could.

The "uncle" kicked me harder.

"What are you doing?" The translator from the first line stepped between us. "Don't kick him again." He pulled me up. I held my side where I'd been kicked and looked at him in surprise. I'd thought he'd forgotten about me. Now he pulled me over beside Giosè. "That isn't his uncle. He just says it because one of his boys is sick and he needs a substitute for the *padrone*."

"The guy says he's the boy's uncle," said Giosè, "so he is."

"Listen to the way he talks. He's from somewhere in Basilicata, but the boy's from Napoli."

"What, do you think I'm deaf?" said Giosè. "You're German; I'm the Italian. This is my country they come from. I hear how they talk. That doesn't change a thing. The boy needs an uncle."

"He's got shoes. He's going to stand right here till his father comes. He's not going anywhere with some fake uncle."

Giosè looked at the "uncle" with both palms turned upward in apology. "Eh, beh, what can you do?" He pointed to the stairs behind him. "Those are the stairs of separation.

67

The sick boy goes in that hall to the left. If you ever want to see him again, you go with him. Everyone else goes down the stairs to fetch baggage and buy ferry tickets." He held his hand out low, at the side of the podium.

The "uncle" put money in Giosè's hand. Then he pushed the feverish boy toward the hall on the left and barked at the rest of the boys to go with him downstairs. The sick boy left without a word. I was sure he believed what he'd said—he was going to the sick home to die. I wanted to yell to him, "Fight!" Hadn't his mother told him to survive?

I didn't want to stand anywhere near Giosè anymore. But where else could I go? The endless lines kept moving.

After about an hour Giosè unwrapped a skinny loaf of bread stuffed with cheese and meats. Lettuce, tomato, onion, and pepper flopped out the sides. He said, "In America they call this an Italian sandwich." He laughed in a chummy way, as though he hadn't just tried to betray me. "These Americans," he said, "they give only an hour for lunch—not enough to get home and eat in pleasure." He shook his head.

His complaints went on and on. Did he think I cared one bit? Did he think he could win me back so easily? I listened because I had to. Otherwise, he might get mad and pawn me off on the next "uncle."

I was hungry for his food, but Jews don't eat cheese and meat together. Still, it looked good. The people in the line glanced at the sandwich, closed their mouths, and looked away.

Giosè stood chewing over me. "Stay here and stand tall while I go eat. Your father will find you soon."

The minute he was gone, I sat on the floor.

A man pushed a metal cart between the lines, selling boxed lunches of sandwiches, fruit, and pie for a half dollar. People paid in their different monies. A box lunch was big enough to feed five men. You could buy bread for four pennies, a sweet cake for six pennies, sausage for ten. I didn't know what the prices meant, and it didn't matter, because I didn't have pennies. But the smells . . .

Finally, Giosè came back. He didn't tell me to stand up. He got back to work.

The German translator said he was leaving for lunch now, and he handed me a piece of newspaper. I unwrapped it. A corner of a sandwich sat there. "Thank you," I said in amazement.

"Don't mention it," he said.

I took out the meat and ate the rest of the sandwich. The meat was pink; it could have been pig. I looked around for a place to stash it so the translator wouldn't find out that I hadn't eaten it. Mamma always said ingrates were the worst kind of people.

I worked the meat inside a pocket. Then I leaned my head against the inspector's podium and fell asleep.

Tap, tap. Someone was tapping on the top of my head.

I looked up into Giosè's face. "The lines are done," he said. "No one reported a lost son. You were a fool not to go with that 'uncle.'" He straightened his cap. "All right, it's time for us to deal with you. Did you come off that ship called *Città di Napoli*?"

I nodded.

The German translator asked, "You're really alone? Like you said?"

I nodded.

He picked up his pen. "What's your last name?"

Could my name get me in trouble? I shrugged.

"I've got to write something. You came over on *Città di Napoli* . . . so, okay, your last name is Napoli."

"Don't do that," said Giosè. "Call him di Napoli or de Napoli or da Napoli—not just Napoli. Only Jews take city names for their last name."

My breath caught. "Napoli is okay with me," I said.

"So you do want to talk," said the German translator. "Good. But Giosè has a point. You don't want to be taken for a Jew, trust me."

Adversity, that was what he was talking about. Like Uncle Aurelio said. I didn't care what adversity I'd face in America. I wasn't going to be here long anyway. And no matter what, I'd always be loyal to my family. "Put my last name as Napoli," I said firmly, feeling Nonna's approval.

He lifted an eyebrow. "All right, Signor Napoli, don't get upset. Anyway, you can use whatever name you want after you leave here. So, what first name do you want?"

I stood there.

"I have to put a first name, or I can't give you the document you need."

"Dom," I said.

"Domenico," he said, writing on a form.

"No, just Dom," I said.

He hesitated. Then he stuck out his bottom lip and nodded. "All right, Napoli, Dom. Birth date?"

"Twenty-fourth of December."

"A Christmas present, huh?" Both men laughed.

"What year?" When I shrugged, he asked, "How old are you?"

"Nine."

"That would make 1883—no, 1882, because you were born at the end of the year. So, who's waiting for you here in New York?"

I shrugged.

"No one? Oh, boy." He put down his pen. "Here's how it works, Dom. Beyond that door you get a physical inspection . . ."

Giosè cut in, "No one's going to let you onto the streets of New York alone. A boy your age needs a family or a *padrone*."

"*Padroni* are illegal," I said defiantly. I could find a policeman and tell him all about the money Giosè took from the "uncles." I could, if I knew where a policeman was. And if a policeman would listen to me. And if he spoke Napoletano. Suddenly it all felt so hard.

"Lots of things are illegal," said Giosè calmly. "The *padroni* have been running the show for years."

"I don't want a *padrone*."

"I don't blame you," said the German translator. "So that means you need a family."

"Change his name to di Napoli," said Giosè, "like I said. The translator in the third line, the one who knows almost no Italian, wrote in di Napoli for at least four men today whose last names he couldn't spell. The kid can try to find one of them and latch on."

The German translator picked up his pen.

"No," I said. "I'll stay Napoli. Napoli, Dom."

"All right, then, kid. It's your life. You'll go it alone. If you act smart, you've got a chance. Others your age have done it." He filled out my form.

"What are you doing?" I asked. "Why are you writing without asking me anything?"

"The whole thing's a lie anyway," said the German translator. "But it's the only way you'll get into Manhattan."

"What's Manhattan?"

"The main part of New York City. Where the big buildings are."

"I don't want to go to New York City," I said. "I want to go to Napoli."

"No one's going to pay your fare back, boy," Giosè said. "It's New York City or an orphanage—your choice."

Orphanages. We had them in Napoli; the nuns ran them. Children who had no one in the world lived there in misery. I saw myself in ragged clothing, covering my ears against Catholic preaching, alone forever. "No."

One of the nurses who had tested me earlier appeared, shaking her head and scolding the men. She grabbed my hand and pulled me away.

Something tugged at the back of my waistband. I felt behind with my hand. Someone had tucked folded sheets of paper into my pants. I quickly jammed them in my pocket.

CHAPTER TEN

Needs

The nurse took me to benches at long tables, where tired people sat. Many had chalk marks on their jackets. She tapped on shoulders, getting everyone to look at me. When no one claimed me, she gestured for me to sit and she marked with chalk on the back of my shirt. I could feel her write a giant *O*.

Every so often, a nurse came up and led someone down the hall to the left. But mostly, we waited. A man pushed a metal cart between the tables and gave crackers to everyone and warm milk to the children. It tasted funny, but I drank it.

Some of us were herded upstairs to dormitory rooms. Triple-decker beds pushed against each other in pairs. I was put in the room with the women and children. We were told to leave our things and come down in two hours to eat. In the meantime we should line up for washing. Mothers stripped their children.

I wasn't about to undress, so I had to find a way to avoid the washing. And I wanted to look at that paper in my pocket.

I went to the bathroom, but women crowded around it. I headed for the stairs down to the bathroom I'd used during the day.

An Italian woman stood in my path arguing with a woman in uniform. "I paid my passage."

"But you came alone," said the official. "And no man is waiting for you."

"See these hands?" The Italian woman held up red hands. "I did laundry night and day to get here."

"Unescorted women are not allowed off Ellis Island. It doesn't matter how many people you argue with, that's the rule. We'll have to contact an immigrant aid society to come get you."

"No charity home. I take care of myself. I have money."

"Don't say it too loud," said the official, "or you soon won't." She fingered the keys that hung from her waist.

"I paid my passage."

"The women's home is nice, I hear." She jiggled her keys.

"I hear it's a hellhole. I paid my passage."

I sidled past them and went downstairs. The bathroom was locked from the inside. I waited.

An official appeared from around the corner. I looked at my feet and hardly breathed. He walked by.

And still no one came out of the bathroom.

Finally I knocked. "Excuse me?"

The door opened a crack. An eye peeked at me. Then a hand grabbed my shirt and pulled me in, locking the door behind me.

We were pressed against each other in the tiny stall. I looked up into a boy's face.

"What are you doing making noise like that, trying to get me in trouble?" He was clearly from Napoli.

"I just want to use the toilet," I said.

"No one's supposed to use this one after hours." He frowned. "Go on."

I hunched over and did my business.

"Hurry up," he said. "And make sure no one sees you leave."

I reached for the doorknob.

"Hold on." He put his hand on my shoulder. "Did you see if the stairs of separation were empty?"

"Are you trying to sneak out?"

His cheek twitched.

"I want to sneak out, too," I said.

"You? What are you, nine? Ten? I'm fourteen. I can do a man's work. I can earn five dollars a week in a textile mill. Or even more. They won't let me work officially till I'm sixteen, but underage workers make it through all the time. I'm going to make it through."

"You'll look older with a little brother tagging along."

He pressed his lips together. "Get out of here."

I opened the door and peeked out.

The boy shut the door, pulling me inside again. "You should have told me you're an orphan."

"Who says I'm an orphan?"

"The *O* on the back of your shirt. Even if you do sneak

through, whoever sees that *O* will turn you in and you'll be thrown into an orphanage. You won't get out till you're sixteen."

I took off my shirt, turned it inside out, and put it on.

"That's too obvious. You need a new shirt. And pants, too. Yours are ripped. Tell you what. I know where you can get other clothes. But you have to promise to bring me back some, too."

"Okay."

"Why should I trust you?"

"Why shouldn't you?"

His forehead furrowed.

"Look," I said. "If I bring back clothes, you're better off. And if I don't, you're no worse off."

He swallowed. "You're too smart for your age."

"I'll bring back clothes," I said. "I owe you for telling me what the *O* meant." And then maybe you'll let me come with you, I thought. But I said, "That way we're even."

"Upstairs there's a room full of used clothes. Get me a coat. And pants and a shirt."

"I can't carry all that. Besides, it's hot out."

"Summer doesn't last forever, kid. It's not like Napoli. It snows here."

Snow? But what did it matter? I'd be home soon. "Where's the room?"

"Somewhere upstairs. Search." He opened the door a crack.

I peeked, then raced up the stairs. I walked near the wall and glanced into open doors.

I came to a closed door. Locked. But the next door opened to reveal piles of clothes. I shut the door behind me. From the window I saw people scurrying about. It would be easy to get lost in that crowd—and then I could figure out what to do next.

Across the water tall buildings rose. A ship docked in the narrows. It looked small from here, a wolf in a canyon. Would I ever see the canyons near Napoli again? Would I ever see Mamma?

Not if they threw me in an orphanage.

I took the papers out of my pocket, finally. They were the documents the German translator had filled out. Somehow they would help me. I changed into a clean short-sleeved shirt and lightweight pants and tucked the papers in my new pocket. Then I grabbed a coat for the boy in the bathroom. I stuffed a shirt for him down one of the coat sleeves and a pair of pants down the other. I took the meat from my old shirt pocket and put it in the coat pocket. The boy could eat it later.

I walked back along the balcony. A hand caught my shoulder, and a woman yanked on the coat. I pulled away and ran. When I snuck a glance back at her, she was watching me.

The boy in the bathroom was waiting. He'd make a dash for it soon. Then I'd be alone again. And someone would write another *O* on my back. And I'd never make it onto a boat. Never get home to Mamma.

I needed something to catch that woman's attention so I could get to the bathroom. Anything.

I took the meat out of the coat pocket and tapped on the shoulder of a man. He looked at me. I pointed at the woman and handed him the meat. The man frowned. He stood up and walked toward her. I forced my way past the rest of the men and ran down the stairs. I tapped on the bathroom door.

The door opened. The boy snatched the coat and shut the door in my face.

Panicked, I dashed down a hall and opened a door.

Men stood with their shirts in their hands, waiting to be inspected. A young girl carried a coffee cup to a doctor. She left through a side door.

A few of the other doctors had cups on the tables near them.

I picked up two empty cups. One in each hand, I walked out the door the girl had used.

I was in a kitchen.

A woman tilted her head at me and said something.

I forced a smile and put the cups on the counter. Then I walked through the kitchen and out another door and, sure enough, there were stairs. I went down and out onto the street.

CHAPTER ELEVEN

Manhattan

I broke out running. I wove in and out of the people, checking over my shoulder. No one had followed me.

Ellis Island was easy to figure out. Ships docked on one side to drop off people. Smaller boats docked on the other to take them away. Immigrants stood in little groups and wrinkled their brows, carefully counting American money. Some were met by the joyous shouts of relatives. Others milled around in the early evening heat with paper pinned to their shirts. They looked hopefully at everyone who passed. A tall man went from person to person, reading their names off those papers. He gathered some together. One man said, "Ah, so you're my *padrone*." After that, anytime I saw someone reading name tags, I hurried the other way.

Women in white uniforms with red crosses on the sleeve gave out doughnuts and apples. They didn't offer me any, so I took two doughnuts off a pile. They weren't nearly so good as *zeppole* back home, but okay. People ate sandwiches the women had given them, but there weren't any left. When I finished the doughnuts, I took an apple. Other women not in uniform but all wearing the same little hats helped people find lost baggage or relatives. America was full of women who wanted to help strangers.

Many spoke languages I understood more or less—Italian dialects, I heard a woman call them. I followed her around for a while, until I heard her explain she was sent by a society to help protect Italian immigrants. I would have asked her what we needed protection against, but I didn't want her to notice me.

A man clutched a scrap of paper and showed it to another man in uniform, who pointed. "That's the boat to Mulberry Street."

Mulberry Street. Napoletani. Maybe Tonino, Mamma's friend. I'd try to get on a ship back to Napoli first, but if I needed help, I'd look for Tonino.

At the boat I walked past the ticket-taker, ready to show the documents in my waistband. But he didn't ask for anything. In Italy, I'd have gotten nabbed by the collar. Here, I was almost invisible. Good. That would make it easy to stow away on a ship back to Napoli when I reached the Manhattan docks.

The ferry left Ellis Island. Seagulls flew alongside. The evening sun seemed to sink into their white feathers and get lost entirely, turning them into flying balls of light. It was the strangest thing, but those seagulls made me happy.

I remembered my last full day in Napoli—how a seagull had watched what the *scugnizzi* were doing, how it had probably been waiting for its chance to steal. It felt like years ago.

We docked at a pier and got off. The press of people during the ferry ride gave way to nothing but a sea breeze at my back. Night was coming, and how I wished I could wrap up in Mamma's shawl. But I'd find a ship to hide on; everything would be okay.

Horses pulled wagons and people pushed carts of all kinds. A fish market was closing, and a man threw buckets of seawater over the wooden planks outside the shop. He scooped a few fish out of a tub of melting ice, the remains of the day, and laid them in a row on the pier. Then he dumped the icy water into the harbor. He went back inside the shop as boys ran up, grabbed the fish, and disappeared down a street. They were naked, but for two in short pants. They'd been swimming. The fishmonger came out, locked his shop, and walked away. He didn't even glance at the pier.

Laying the fish side by side like that, so neat and clean, had been a gift to the poor. And women gave out apples and doughnuts on Ellis Island, even if the doughnuts tasted pretty bad. Maybe everyone in America took care of the poor.

A lamplighter worked his way along the road. People left the wharf area and seeped back into the innards of the city. I ducked into a side street. A man turned the corner up ahead and walked toward me with a dog. I darted down an alley.

There was excrement everywhere, from dogs and cats

and horses. And from people. The walls stank of urine. A rat shrieked and ran by with another one chasing it.

I ran out onto the next street. Stay out of alleys! And there was the man from the ferry, the one who wanted Mulberry Street. I followed him. I could wait till morning to find a ship. For now I needed a place to sleep.

A coach rolled past, pulled by two horses. Men with an air of importance sat tall on its benches, wearing black hats. They knew exactly where they were going, where they belonged.

I held the hem of my shirt in my fists and squeezed tight. I wanted to stop and lie down. Exhaustion washed over me.

The man I was following stopped, asked directions, and got pointed along. Cafe tables and chairs cluttered the sidewalks, where people ate and talked under round lanterns. Spicy aromas circled them.

A woman passed with a cloth sack over her shoulder and a pig at her heels. She stooped to pick up a bottle and slide it into the sack as the pig trotted to a garbage can. Together they sorted through the stinking waste.

I hurried to keep within sight of the man. He turned right, went a few blocks, then turned left. He knocked on a door and people rushed out to surround him. A smell came with them—porcini mushrooms and garlic and rosemary and tomatoes. They all talked at once: "Giorgio was supposed to go meet you, but he got the day wrong." "Sorry, sorry." "Now you're here and everything will be good." They rushed him inside.

The door closed. The dinner smell faded.

I stood there. On Mulberry Street. My bottom lip trembled.

A rock hit me on the shoulder. I went to grab it and throw it back, but it was a rock-hard dog turd. I almost fell on it, I was so surprised.

A boy a few years older than me stood at the opening of an alley. "Get out of here."

I walked up the sidewalk fast, checking over my shoulder for him. I crossed a street and a man pushing a cart had to swerve around me, cursing. Things fell off his cart. I stooped to help pick them up, but he shouted at me, "Thief!"

A woman yelled, "For shame! Think of your mother. Think how humiliated she'd be."

I ran to her. "Do you know Tonino?"

"Which Tonino?"

"The widower. He left his children in Napoli."

"Go home," she said over her shoulder as she walked off.

It was dark by then and I wanted to run away. I turned around and went back to the alley where the boy had stood. After all, that boy looked just as alone as me.

He was gone.

"Where are you?" I tried not to step in anything putrid, calling, calling. I crossed a street and went up the next alley. It was slow going because of all the garbage. And it wasn't just garbage. The carcass of a big dog lay to one side. The smell was awful. I remembered the body in the grotto back home and cleansing myself of that stench in the lake on Vesuvio. Nowhere to wash here.

Then I saw the boy up ahead. I walked more quickly. So did a man in uniform. He blew a whistle. The boy ran and the policeman ran after him.

Nothing was going right. I had no new plans—me, the boy full of plans. I went back to the alley with the dead dog. I threw pieces of a crushed wooden box into a half-empty barrel to make a clean layer on top of whatever was inside. Then I climbed in. I looked up to say good night to the stars, but I couldn't see any. At home, no stars meant rain was on the way.

I checked to make sure the documents were safe in my pocket. Then I recited every one of Nonna's charms I could remember—charms to keep evil at bay.

That was where I spent my first night in America, grateful for the exhaustion that let me sleep. If there was one lesson I'd learned since I left Mamma, it was to sleep: sleep puts aside cares.

CHAPTER TWELVE

Sharks and Mooks

I woke to the noise of horses on cobblestone streets.

My neck hurt from being bent over my knees for hours. I stood and picked a chicken bone off my pants. It had jabbed my thigh all night, but I'd been too afraid of what it might be to touch it.

Rain started, turning the gray alley stones to black. It was just a drizzle and it felt good. I climbed out onto a log that rolled out from under me. I fell onto my bottom with a smack.

I brushed off everywhere and rubbed my shoes with the underside of the front of my shirt. Then I raised my face to the rain, mouth open. The fat, slow drops soothed my cheeks and throat. A high-pitched tinkling came, so delicate I thought I was still dreaming. I followed it.

A bony boy walked down the sidewalk beating a

metal triangle with a rod. Other people were out on the sidewalk already, too, heads bowed under kerchiefs and hats. Some carried umbrellas. Whenever the boy passed someone, he beat the triangle louder, then put out his hand. A man gave him a coin.

He was nothing but a beggar.

The beggar boy went slowly, so I had a chance to look around. Windows were open everywhere. People lived crowded together as in Napoli—filling basements and garrets, as well as all the floors between. A man came out of an outhouse, and the way he stretched, I knew he'd spent the night there.

I gritted my teeth. I wouldn't sleep in a barrel again. I wasn't a *scugnizzo*.

By the time the beggar boy finally stopped on a corner, the rain had let up. Early sun glinted off the wet stones. Too bad I hadn't stood in one spot and drunk the rain while it was still coming down. My throat was dry.

The beggar boy took a tin cup out of his pocket, put it on the ground, and played his triangle. Then he whistled a tune. Men dressed in fancy suits dropped in coins.

"Hey," I said to him.

He turned his back to me. He was pretty tall, but I bet he was only a year older than me.

"Hey, can you tell me which way to the boats to Napoli?"

"*Bolivia,*" said the beggar boy. He pointed.

Soon I was out on the wharves again, where a huge passenger ship was docked. Officials on the steerage deck processed the first- and second-class passengers.

I walked around until I found two men talking Napoletano while they laid bricks in a sidewalk.

"Excuse me. Do you know about the *Bolivia*?"

The younger man jerked his chin toward the dock. "That ship?"

"Is it going to Napoli?"

"It just came from there," said the other man. "No one cares where it's going next."

"I do," the younger man said. "In Italy the air is *bell' e fresca*—clear and cool. I'm going back as soon as I make enough money."

"Yeah?" said the other man. "You'll take one whiff and you'll be on the next boat back to America, like every other fool who forgot what Italy's really like."

"I'm going back to Italy," I said.

The man wiped his mustache. "Get a load of this kid," he said to the younger man. "Talks like a big shot."

"It's true," I said.

"Don't let your mother hear you say that," said the younger man. "You'll break her heart."

"My mother's in Italy."

"Where's your father?" said the other man.

I didn't answer.

"You alone?"

"Not for long," I said. "I'm going to sneak onto that ship."

"You'll never make it," said the man. "See the guards?"

"And if you get caught trying," said the younger man, "you'll wind up in an orphanage."

"Orphanages aren't as bad as the streets," said the other man.

"Remember that one that burned down? Half a dozen kids died."

A shopkeeper came outside and said something to the men in English. They got back to work.

If my experience on the last passenger ship was typical, it would be a long time before the *Bolivia* was empty and I could sneak on. Days, probably. So I walked along the wharf toward the Statue of Liberty.

A ferry crossed from Ellis Island. My eyes fixed on it. There was no one aboard I could know, no long-lost cousin. But I stood watching anyway.

A man got off and went up to a policeman and asked him something. The policeman answered in English. The man got so flustered, he pulled a piece of cigar from his pocket and fiddled with it. The policeman took out a match and lit the man's cigar. The man's face widened in a huge smile of surprise. I was smiling, too. For this moment it didn't matter that no one understood anyone else.

A group of men came up to the policeman now. They said the same words over and over, till I found myself whispering them, too—the English words: "Which way Lester Brothers?" The policeman turned to other passing men, and more people got consulted, and soon there was a crowd.

An Italian said to another man, "Ignorant Irish. They want to make shoes at the Lester Brothers factory, and they don't even know it's way out in Binghamton. Days away."

"Someone ought to tell them to go over to Chatham Square to earn the travel money to get to Binghamton," said the other man.

"You going to tell them? You going to help the Irish?"

They laughed and went on.

And just like that I had my next plan. I'd work in

Chatham Square till the *Bolivia* was empty and I could sneak on. But first I had to get breakfast. Where were the American ladies who liked to help strangers? No one handed out food on this wharf.

I went back up the street. It was busier now; skinny children in rags hawked their wares. Their dirty hair was blond or light brown, their faces red and snot-streaked. They had scabs and open sores on their elbows and knees.

The beggar boy with the triangle stood on the same corner. "Have you got anything to eat?" I asked him.

He turned away and whistled again, the same tune as before. Someone dropped a coin into his tin cup.

What a stupid question. Maybe a night in a barrel had softened my brains.

Okay, so there was no food sitting around for the taking. That meant a job came first, then breakfast. "Which way Chatham Square?" I asked him, using the English I'd heard from the men who came off the ferry—my very first attempt.

He spat on the ground in front of me.

"Come on," I pleaded in Napoletano. "I need to get to Chatham Square."

"So what," he said in English. I didn't understand, of course, and he knew that. After a bit, he said in Napoletano, "Why?"

"I need money."

"You, begging? With those fancy shoes?" He spat again. "Forget it. That area's taken. And the *padrone* in charge of those boys will whip you bloody if you move in."

"I'm going to work, not beg," I said.

"So what," he said again in English. Then he shook his

head. "You think I don't work? I stand here all day long. I have to bring in eighty cents or my *padrone* will beat me."

"Why don't you run away?"

"He binds our wrists to the bedpost at night."

I looked around. No one was watching this boy, so far as I could see. "Why don't you run away right now?"

"Think you're so smart, do you? Where would I go? Anyway, I owe him money. And this is work. Decent work. There's no crime in being poor."

"That's the truth." Everyone I'd ever known was poor. "But begging . . ." I didn't finish.

"I make music. It's not the same as begging. I give people what they want to hear. What's the matter with you? You don't recognize 'Daisy Bell'? The new song about the bicycle built for two?" He whistled the tune again. Someone dropped a coin in his cup. He whistled another tune. Another person dropped in a coin. He gave me a self-satisfied look. "That was 'After the Ball Is Over.' You don't know that one, either, do you? It's the most popular song from Tin Pan Alley." His last three words were in English.

"What's Tin Pan Alley?"

"Twenty-eighth Street. Where they write the songs."

I shrugged. "I've never been there."

"So what," he said in English. His mouth twitched. "I've never been there, either. But everyone knows the songs."

I shrugged again.

He pressed his lips together. "It's okay. I wouldn't actually know about them myself if the woman downstairs didn't sing them half the night. You need money, huh? Tell you what. Give me those shoes to hold for you, and you can take my corner and play this triangle. As soon as you've got

90

a dollar, I'll split the extra twenty cents with you, half and half."

That was how I learned that a dollar was one hundred cents. "No," I said.

"That's ten cents each."

"I can count."

"You'd get the money fast. They always give more to smaller boys. And you're clean. You'd be done by afternoon."

Me, clean? Nonna would be appalled at how filthy I'd gotten. "I won't take off my shoes."

"Then they won't give you nothing. You got to look poor."

"There's no way I'll beg."

His cheeks flushed. "You don't listen good." He spat. "So what," he said in English. "No one cares what you think."

"Which way Chatham Square?" I said jokingly, trying to make up.

"Get out of here. You'd only get me in trouble with my *padrone* anyway." He pointed. "Turn right at Park." And he went back to playing his triangle.

"Thanks," I said.

He turned his back on me and whistled that second tune.

I walked the way he'd pointed. At every corner I asked, "Park?" After several blocks someone finally nodded yes. I looked at the street sign. *P-A-R-K*. That was how you spelled *park*. It was almost the same as how I'd have spelled those sounds in Italian. In the top right corner of the sign were the letters *S-T*. Could that be a word?

I turned right. It wasn't long before I was passing all kinds of factories. They made silverware, jewelry, billiard tables. They made umbrellas, lightning rods, false teeth, paper, medicines, guns. I passed a piano factory and a carriage factory and one for ship propellers. I stood outside the windows and watched and listened. I heard so many languages, even one that sounded sort of like singing, out of the mouths of gaunt men wearing funny quilted jackets in a cigar factory. But no one spoke Italian.

It didn't seem possible. I knew where Chatham Square was—I'd passed Mulberry Street to get here, so it was right at the bottom of the street where all the Italians lived. Where were the Italian workers?

A boy stood on a corner with a tin cup on the ground. He played a small harp. I went up to him. "Where are the factories that Italians work in?"

He turned his back to me. Red welts showed under the collar of his shirt. I stepped away in a hurry, praying his *padrone* hadn't seen me, that I hadn't gotten him in trouble.

I hurried to Mulberry Street and went up the block, past the hanging sides of beef and pork in front of the butcher's, past the pharmacy, past the ratcatcher who stood by a wall, holding out a string with dead rats attached by the tail. He was good! I hurried along listening for someone I could talk to, anyone who could explain how I could earn money.

And he appeared, the boy who had thrown the dog turd at me the night before. He stepped out of an alley into my path, legs planted. "I told you to get out of here."

"I'm glad the policeman didn't catch you," I said.

"How'd you know about the policeman?"

I shrugged. "I need to find a factory with Italian work-ers so I can earn money."

"That why you were in Chatham Square?"

"How'd you know I was there?"

He crossed his arms on his chest. "Even if you weren't a little squirt, you couldn't get a job there. Chatham Square factory managers don't hire from this neighborhood. They think they're too good for Five Points people. Italians can only work laying bricks or breaking stones or digging ditches."

"What are you talking about?"

"You don't know anything, do you?" The tough guy walked around me. "Where'd you get those shoes?"

"My mother bought them for me."

"Where's your mother?"

"At home."

"Where's home?"

I shrugged.

"I bet you live in Brooklyn, and you got lost in the city, right? So now you want to do some piddling errand so you can make enough money to take the streetcar home. Or, no, you live in the Bronx, that's it, right? The Italians in the Bronx make good. That's how your mamma got money for those shoes." He smirked. "That, or she works at home."

"Of course she works at home," I said. "She helps Aunt Sara with laundry and mending."

He laughed. "You really know nothing. That's not what 'working at home' means. You want to know how to get a job?" He leaned toward me and beckoned with a curled finger.

I stepped forward.

"Turn Irish," he whispered.

"Irish? How?"

He laughed again. "You don't. You can't turn white just by wishing. Irish boys get all the bootblack jobs. They deliver all the newspapers. There's no way an Italian boy like you can get a penny without begging or stealing. And if you beg around here, the *padroni* will beat you to a pulp. They own every street corner worth begging on. And if you steal, you have to give half of everything to me."

"I don't steal. And I'd never beg. And why would I have to give you half, anyway?"

"So I wouldn't turn you in. That's how it works."

My stomach hurt. "I'm hungry."

"Who isn't? Give me your shoes and I'll give you fare for the streetcar."

I knew what a streetcar was. They were building one in Milano, up in the north of Italy. Uncle Aurelio had talked about it.

"My shoes wouldn't fit you," I said.

"You think I'd want to wear them? I'd sell them in a second."

"If I wanted to ride a streetcar, I'd sell them myself," I said.

"You don't know who to sell them to," said the boy. "I do."

I walked around him. I passed a shoemaker and a barbershop and a candy maker, and from each of their doorways I heard Italian. So that boy was wrong. Italians could get jobs—at least on Mulberry Street.

A produce vendor was taking oranges from a bushel

basket and arranging them in piles on a low table outside his shop. "Want me to do that for you?" I asked.

He glanced at me. "Go home."

I stepped closer. "It'll only cost you an orange."

"Didn't you hear me? Don't bother me. Don't bother my customers." He didn't speak Napoletano, but I could understand him pretty well. And his tone wasn't mean, just wary.

"You've got better things to do," I said. "And I can do it perfect."

"Perfect?" He looked at me again, amused.

I made a circle of my thumb and index finger and drew my hand across the air in front of my chest in the gesture that meant *perfect*.

Was he almost smiling?

I lifted my chin and looked straight into his eyes, hopeful.

"What do you know about stacking fruit, a little kid like you?"

"If you don't like the job I do, you don't pay me."

"If I turn around and you run off with an orange in each hand, I'll come after you and make you sorry you were ever born."

"I don't steal."

He pushed the bushel of oranges toward me. "You get a tomato, not an orange," he said.

So I stacked the oranges, the way I stacked Nonna's yarn balls at home. I was careful; not a single orange rolled away. I imagined Nonna watching me, saying some proverb—maybe the one about how the eye had to have its part in everything. That was why it was worth it to make even the smallest thing beautiful, even a plate of food that would be eaten in an instant. I stacked the oranges for Nonna's sake.

The man was standing behind me when I finished. "Do these tomatoes and the zucchini and the onions, and I'll give you two tomatoes."

Amazed, I stacked them just right. "Can I come back tomorrow?"

"Sure, but it's Sunday. I'll be closed. Here." He handed me a bruised orange, as well as two tomatoes.

"I wonder, do you know a widower named Tonino?"

The man shook his head.

I put the food in my pocket and walked back to the mouth of the alley. I knew the tough guy would show up sooner or later.

It was sooner.

Before he could speak, I handed him a tomato—a tomato my own mouth was watering to eat.

"That's right," he said. "Half of everything."

"I didn't steal them," I said. "And I didn't give you one because you said I should. I gave you one 'cause I wanted to."

He looked me up and down. Then he leaned over and bit his tomato. Juice squirted out and landed on my shoe.

"Watch it!" I pushed him away, squatted, and wiped off the mess with the hem of my shirt.

When I stood again, he stuffed the rest of the tomato in his mouth and grinned as he chewed. "I knew it. You wouldn't sell those shoes no matter what. What were they, a birthday present?"

I ate my tomato.

"So why'd you want to give me a tomato, then?"

I thought of how Nonna had made me bring the bowl of meatballs to the Rossi family next door the night before I left home. "You get, you give."

"*Magari.* What gave you such an idea? Look at you: the king of Mulberry Street, just giving things out right and left. Well, listen good. In this neighborhood it's everybody for himself."

Magari. I had to shut my eyes hard against the surge of longing; I could see Nonna sitting at the kitchen table sighing, "*Magari.*" I could smell her garlic hands, see the thick knobs of her knuckles. And now I realized I'd given this guy the tomato for another reason, too. Mamma said survive. This guy could be an ally. As Nonna's proverb went: "*A chi me dà pane io 'o chiamme pate*"—Anyone who feeds me is like a father to me.

I took out the orange and peeled it. It smelled like flowers. The boy watched me closely. Before I had a chance to think, I gave him half and ate a section of my half. It tasted wonderful. Juicy.

He ate his orange fast. "So you think you're a big guy 'cause some jerk from Calabria paid you, huh? Big deal, tomatoes cost next to nothing. And that orange was too bruised to sell. You still don't have your streetcar fare."

I finished my part of the orange and licked my fingers. This guy was older than me, but he wasn't that tough. The way he devoured the food told me that. Really tough guys were never that hungry—not in Napoli. A bad guy would have simply knocked me down and stolen my shoes. "I don't want money. I just want enough food to last me two days."

"Two days. I'm supposed to put up with you for two days?"

My heart banged; I could stay with him. "Yeah. Where do you sleep?"

"Whoa. You're not sleeping anywhere near me. And don't ask where I sleep. Look. I like being alone. There are gangs of boys around here—but they're always noticed, so they're always getting in trouble. I stay alone, and I don't stay in one place too long, so no one hassles me. The most I'll do is look out for you. But if you want my protection, you're going to have to show you're worth it."

"How?" I said.

"In the next block Pasquale Cuneo runs a salami shop. Go do a chore for him, and bring me back prosciutto—the raw kind."

Prosciutto was pig meat. "No."

"Don't make me mad, kid."

That was the last thing I wanted to do. "What's your name?" I asked.

"What's yours?"

"Dom."

"Mine's Gaetano."

"I can do lots of work, Gaetano. But not in a shop that sells pig meat."

"Why not?"

I shrugged.

"If you don't do what I say, you'll be alone. You can't make it alone. Not in Five Points."

I was sick of being alone. It couldn't be that bad to be around pig meat, so long as I didn't eat it. "I'll do it."

"You bet you will. You're lucky it's a slow day, or I wouldn't pay any attention to you at all. Understand?"

"Yeah."

Gaetano rubbed his mouth in thought. "Okay. I got a better idea. On Park Street there's a big store run by Luigi Pierano. He's got every kind of Italian food." He slapped me on the back. "Go work for him and bring me four pennies."

I wanted to ask him to show me a penny, so I'd be sure to bring him what he wanted. But then he'd know I wasn't from that place he said—the Bronx. I felt safer having him think I had a mother close by who might show up on a streetcar at any minute.

I turned around and went back to Park Street. There were lots of stores with writing on the windows. None of them had the name Luigi Pierano. But one was bigger than most. I went in.

Rows of shelves from floor to ceiling brimmed over with food. A line of bins held spices. I stood over the one with the seeds I knew so well—anise—and breathed deeply. Mamma's scent. For an instant the room swirled and my head went light.

A woman clamped a hand around my upper arm and steadied me. She said something in English, then in some Italian dialect, "Are you ill?" I smiled to reassure her. She walked on.

A man behind the counter was making gigantic sandwiches. A card taped to the front of the counter read 25¢. Twenty-five cents? Was it a lot?

"Can I do a chore for you?" I asked the sandwich maker.

"Get out of here." He didn't even look at me. His tone was final.

I went outside. A crowd had gathered at the foot of the next street. I crossed Park and worked my way between the adults to the inside of the circle. An organ grinder played music and a monkey on a chain took off his cap to people in the crowds.

The woman beside me put a coin in the monkey's cap. The monkey's tiny, long fingers clasped around her thumb for a shake. She gasped. The monkey chattered, showing sharp teeth. His eyes darted around with a quick intelligence that made my stomach sick. He knew he was a prisoner and he hated all these people; I could have sworn it.

Everyone took out coins; they all wanted to shake the monkey's hand.

I pushed my way back through the people, bursting free onto the street, and ran the path I'd already traveled twice that day, back toward the boy with the triangle. He was still on the corner. "How much have you gotten?" I asked.

He turned his back to me.

I moved around in front of him. "I asked how much you've gotten."

"So what."

"Listen, Tin Pan Alley, I'll do it. I'll play the triangle."

Tin Pan Alley put his hand in his pocket and counted the coins. "Thirty-two cents," he said. "You have to make sixty-eight more. Then we split the last twenty. Promise?"

"I promise." I took off my shoes; then I suddenly clutched them to my chest. "If you run off with my shoes, I'll catch you," I said. "I'm fast."

"If you run off with my triangle," he said, "my *padrone* will catch you. You can't hide from him."

"I don't steal," I said for the third time that morning.

"You think I do?" Tin Pan Alley stiffened.

I shook my head. He was too proud to steal. I handed him my shoes.

He handed me the triangle. "You smell like oranges." His face looked wistful for a moment. "Play."

I tapped the little metal rod against the triangle. Most people walked by quickly, not looking at me. But whenever someone looked, I smiled big, and, more often than not, they dropped a coin in the tin cup.

Tin Pan Alley sat with his back against the nearest lamp-post and kept an eye out. If he saw his *padrone* coming, he was going to jump up, throw me my shoes, and grab the triangle. I was supposed to run as fast as I could. And if the *padrone* caught me, I was supposed to tell him I worked for someone else; no *padrone* would beat a boy who belonged to another. Instead, he'd take whatever I had and send me on my way with a warning.

The very idea of his *padrone* made me queasy. But I didn't want to be alone again that night, and I didn't see any other way of getting four pennies for Gaetano.

Every so often Tin Pan Alley came over and emptied the tin cup. It had to stay close to empty or no one would give.

People ate as they walked along—ugly meat sticks that Tin Pan Alley called wienerwursts—German food. Sometimes the meat was covered in a stinking rotten cabbage. And they ate sandwiches, much smaller than the ones back in the store on Park Street.

The tomato and the orange half had made me hungrier. The sun was hot. The rumble of horses and carts hammered in my head. I felt woozy and smiled weakly at everyone, whether they looked at me or not.

Tin Pan Alley jiggled his cup in my face. "Ninety-eight cents already. You're good at this, and you don't even whistle. Usually it's slow on Saturdays."

Saturday. It was Saturday. The Sabbath. Jews didn't work on the Sabbath.

But I'd already arranged the fruit. That was work, because the man had paid me.

In fruit, not money. That's not really pay—that's not really work.

And playing music, that wasn't really work, either. It was entertainment. So long as I didn't pocket any of the money. "I'm stopping," I said.

"You look sick." Tin Pan Alley counted out nine coins. "Here's your nine cents."

I shook my head.

"That's half of eighteen," said Tin Pan Alley, "which is what's left over after I pay my *padrone*. I'm not cheating you. You'd have had to get a whole dollar to earn ten cents."

"I told you, I can count," I said.

"So you're trying to cheat me now, is that it? And I thought you were okay. Well, you can't have ten cents. You can't cheat me."

"I'd never cheat you," I said. "I keep a promise. Look, how about you do me a four-cent favor."

"What's that mean?" asked Tin Pan Alley.

"Come with me to Mulberry Street to give a boy four cents."

"Why don't you give him four cents yourself?"

"I can't."

"Why not?"

"I don't want to tell you."

Tin Pan Alley looked at me with troubled eyes.

"Come on, Tin Pan Alley. If you do this, you get to keep my other five cents."

Tin Pan Alley put the coins back in his pocket. "Let's hurry. If my *padrone* passes and finds I'm missing, he'll be mad."

I thought of the welts on the neck of the boy who played the harp in Chatham Square. "How often does he come by?"

"Most days not at all. Other days he'll come a few times. But never early in the morning. Besides that, you can't predict. That way he keeps us honest."

"Mulberry isn't that close," I said. "It'll take time."

"I know where Mulberry is."

"Look, let's not risk trouble with your *padrone*. Just keep the money."

"What, are you feeling sorry for me? Don't waste your time. I'm going to earn back what my *padrone* paid for my passage over and then I'll find a regular job and I'll send to Italy for my aunt and my cousins on Vico Sedil Capuano. We'll all have the good life." He started up the road.

Vico Sedil Capuano. I knew that street. Tin Pan Alley's family was practically my neighbor. What had happened to his parents?

"Come on," he called to me. "A deal's a deal. You think you're the only person in the world who can keep a promise?"

We went to Mulberry Street, to the alley where Gaetano had shown up before, and waited.

"You got the four cents?"

I turned around. Gaetano stood there. Tin Pan Alley put four cents in Gaetano's hand.

"Wait a minute," said Gaetano. "I've got a treat in mind, and it's four cents just for the two of us. I'm not paying for this mook."

"I don't take nothing from no shark," said Tin Pan Alley.

I didn't know what a mook or a shark was, but I could tell they were insults. "Tin Pan Alley," I said quickly, "meet Gaetano. He's my friend. Gaetano, meet Tin Pan Alley. He keeps his promise."

"Oh, another good boy, like you," said Gaetano. "A beggar, huh?"

Tin Pan Alley spat on the ground.

I moved between them. "He's a musician."

"A musician? Not a beggar, just a really skinny musician." Gaetano blew through his lips, making a horse noise. "Well, come on, then." He walked and talked, pointing as we went. "This is Baxter Street. Lots of people from Napoli live here. Like on Mulberry and Mott Streets. But the people from Genova live here, too. And the best ice cream vendor in all of Five Points is here." He led us past grocery stores with wooden barrels of dried fish—delicious *baccalà*—and up to the ice cream vendor. He put the four pennies in the man's hand.

"It's a penny a serving," the man said in his dialect. "You want three extra-large servings for four cents?"

"No. Two doubles," said Gaetano, talking in the same

dialect the ice cream vendor used, "for me and the little squirt." He jerked his elbow toward me. "Nothing for the mook."

"One double," I said. "And two regulars."

The ice cream vendor raised his eyebrows at Gaetano. Gaetano gave me a look of disgust. "I had a big lunch, but I guess I can stuff down a triple serving," he said to the man. "Give the squirt one regular serving, then."

The man took out a bit of brown paper and put a dab of ice cream on it and handed it to me. He gave three dabs to Gaetano.

What Gaetano had done was lousy.

I ate half the ice cream as slowly as I could. It was creamy and cold and not nearly enough. "You could buy a serving," I said to Tin Pan Alley. He had fourteen extra pennies in his pocket, after all—his nine and my five.

"It's not your business what I buy or don't buy," said Tin Pan Alley.

There must have been days when he didn't take in eighty cents. When extra money saved from a good day could spare him a beating.

I handed the paper to Tin Pan Alley.

He ate the rest of the ice cream in one bite and licked the paper clean. Then he turned and walked down Baxter toward Park.

"Bye," I called.

In answer, he looked back over his shoulder at me.

"Where'd you pick him up?" asked Gaetano.

I shrugged. "What's a mook?"

"An idiot."

"He's not an idiot."

"He's got a *padrone,* doesn't he?" asked Gaetano. "Any kid who's owned by a *padrone* is an idiot. If you weren't one to start, you become one fast."

"What's a shark?"

"A boss."

"It can't mean just that," I said. "A boss isn't something bad, but a shark is."

"Depends on how you look at it. A shark sees what there is for the taking and takes it. Sharks are smart." Gaetano pointed at the doors we passed. "That watchmaker, he's a banker on the side. He takes in Italians' money and saves it for them until they've got enough to send for relatives back home. Or, for the really stupid ones, until they think they've made their fortune and decide to go back to Italy. But in the meantime, he gives them nothing—not a cent—and he has their money to use however he wants. He can spend it to start a business of his own. Or he can lend it to immigrants who want to start businesses. None of the real banks will lend them money. But a shark will. He does nothing—he just sits there and makes money off the hard work of the people he lends to. And he makes money off the savings of other people, see? That's a smart shark." He pointed. "That wine store, it's the Banca Italiana. It has no license, nothing. The owner did nothing but say he was running a bank, and people gave him their money. That's what I'm going to do when I get it all together. I'll open a bank."

"And who's going to trust you with their money?" I said.

"You. And mooks like you."

"I'm not a mook."

"Oh, right, you're a king, the way you gave Tin Pan

Alley the rest of your ice cream. Listen, mook. Half-wits like you can't protect yourselves. It's either give me your money or get robbed on the street." Gaetano tilted his head at me. "You keep surprising me, Dom. You know less than the Baxter monkeys."

"I saw a monkey today," I said.

"You like monkeys? That figures. Come on." Gaetano swaggered up the street like a big man—a shark—and I followed like a mook. He stopped midblock. "Here it is. The most famous monkey-training school in the city. A smart monkey goes for thirty dollars." He grinned at me. "You'd go for maybe twenty."

There were curtains over the windows, so I couldn't see inside, thankfully. But I could hear monkey chatter from within. And I heard something else, too. Snaps. A whip?

It was right then that my stomach cramped. I doubled over.

Gaetano laughed. "The price of ice cream," he said. "The Genovesi are pigs. They use dirty ingredients and dirty mixing bowls and they make dirty ice cream. But it tastes the best. If you stick around long enough, your guts'll get used to it."

CHAPTER THIRTEEN

Church

I knew Gaetano was following me. And he knew I knew. He didn't even try to hide. Every time I'd look back over my shoulder, he'd be there, a half block behind.

I didn't go to him, though, no matter how much I wanted company. The ice cream had taught me a lesson. Anyone who would let me get that sick couldn't be trusted. Mamma was right—Eduardo was right—no one could be trusted.

Except maybe Tin Pan Alley; Tin Pan Alley was a stand-up kind of guy. But he was off somewhere with his *padrone*.

So I walked up and down alleys, relieving myself whenever the cramps from the ice cream were too great, never stopping for longer than that, trying to lose Gaetano.

After a while, I stumbled the two blocks east to Elizabeth Street, where Gaetano told me the Siciliani lived. He followed. But when I went beyond that, he stopped and turned around.

I got scared: was something awful east of Elizabeth Street? After all, Gaetano seemed to know everything. I turned back.

And there he was, waiting for me. He followed. Four blocks west of Baxter he stopped again. So I turned back.

Then I went south. Gaetano didn't cross Park. But I knew there was nothing dangerous south of Park, because I'd gone all the way to the wharves.

That meant Gaetano was like the stray dogs back in Napoli. He had a territory. If I slept outside his territory, he couldn't bother me.

But the only place I knew to sleep in was my barrel. I wandered south of Park, until I felt sure he'd given up. Then I snuck back to my barrel.

Sunday morning announced itself with church bells. For a moment I thought I was home in Napoli. Those could have been the bells of San Domenico Maggiore or Cappella San Severo or the Duomo itself.

I thought of that last morning in Napoli. Mamma's black hair, spread across my arm. The smell of meatballs and citronella candles. Sneaking out. I remembered other mornings, too. Her constant singing. Her hand on my cheek. How she lifted me to touch the *mezuzah*.

I didn't cry, though. I didn't make any noise at all,

nothing to let anyone know where I was. Napoli was a dreamworld. I was here. In America. In my barrel.

I had to make sure Gaetano didn't see me getting out of the barrel. I peeked over the edge. An old woman with a sack thrown across her back rummaged at the opening of the alley, putting bones in the sack. When she saw me, she ran off.

This area was filled with ragpickers. Most were women or boys who worked for a *padrone*, picking up junk. I'd seen them the day before.

I jumped out of the barrel and ran all the way to the wharf.

The top deck of the *Bolivia* was empty. The third-class passengers must have been taken to Ellis Island fast. Or maybe the *Bolivia* only had first and second class.

I ran to the plank.

A man came down, addressing me in English.

"I need a job on your ship," I said. "I can do anything and everything. I'll be the errand boy. Everyone's job will be easier with me around."

"Italian?" he said in English. Then he tried to shoo me away.

I stood my ground.

He said more things. Louder.

I wouldn't leave.

He waved over someone from across the street. A policeman.

Okay, keep calm, I told myself. Walk, don't run. Like when a dog's coming at you. I walked along the wharf road without looking back.

I crossed the road and went back up to the neighborhood Gaetano called Five Points.

Gaetano appeared in my path almost immediately. I knew he would. He looked cleaner than usual. His hair was slicked down and the crust he'd had on his chin the day before was gone. "I've been looking for you. It's time to go to church."

"I don't go to church."

"Don't say that." Gaetano hit me on the ear. "Don't ever say that." He walked ahead up Mulberry Street. "Come on."

I didn't move.

"Come on," he said. "There's food."

"Why would you care if I get food?"

"I'll get more if you're with me. Come on, don't be a mook."

I caught up to him.

Gaetano looked down his nose at me. "Yesterday you told that mook we were friends. So are you my friend or not?"

We walked.

"Speak up. Are you my friend or my enemy?"

"I'm not your enemy," I said.

He grinned. Gaetano was the biggest grinner I'd ever met. "Then when I say 'Come,' you come. *Chi me vô bene appriesso me vene.*"

I knew that proverb—If you like me, you follow me. It seemed strange that someone as young as Gaetano would recite proverbs. He was trying to make himself seem important again. "How come you never leave this area?" I asked.

He smirked. "You think you're smart. You think you're smarter than people who are a lot older than you."

I shrugged.

"Like I said, you know nothing. You want to get sick on meat from a Polish butcher, huh? Or fish from a Yiddish fish peddler?"

"What do *Polish* and *Yiddish* mean?"

"Dirty. Polish people come from Poland. Yiddish people come from Germany and other places. Some of the Poles are Jews and all of the Yids are. If you go outside Five Points, who knows what they'll feed you. You'll get sick as a dog."

Jews, dirty? Never. "Sick as I got from that Italian ice cream?"

"Don't be disloyal to Italians," said Gaetano.

That stung. Nonna had always prized loyalty. She said the worst thing you could do was leave someone you loved hanging in the wind.

But I didn't want to give Gaetano the satisfaction of agreeing with him. "Yesterday you said the Genovesi were pigs."

"Between you and me, sure. Among the Napoletani, you can criticize the people from Genova all you want. But don't ever criticize them to people who aren't Italian. Loyalty is more important than anything else."

There was something about his voice that made him seem younger than he was. I felt bolder. "So you stay within Five Points so you won't get sick from Jewish food?" I said. "I don't believe you. I think you're afraid. You're a rabbit."

"Me, a rabbit? It has nothing to do with being afraid. Have you talked to anyone out there?"

"I talked to a ship captain just this morning." Maybe the man I talked to wasn't the captain, but it sounded good.

"In Napoletano?"

"Well, sure. I spoke Napoletano."

"What did he speak?"

"English."

"How's your English?" asked Gaetano.

"Which way Chatham Square?" I said in English. I expected him to laugh.

He looked stricken. "Where'd you learn that? You go to school, huh? All the Italian kids in the Bronx go to school?"

"Those are the only English words I know."

"You swear?"

What was he all worked up about? "Of course."

"You better not be making fun of me."

"I'm not."

"Don't make fun of me ever." Gaetano threw back his shoulders.

"I don't make fun of anyone," I said quietly.

"If you're my friend, you don't make fun of me. Ever."

"I won't. Ever."

He looked around; then he turned back to me. "So that's all the English you know?"

"That's it."

"Well, once you try to say other things, you'll see. Go outside Five Points and people laugh at how you talk."

"How do you know? You don't go outside."

"I hear the Five Points men complaining," he said. "That's why they only work for other Italians."

"They can't work in Chatham Square because they don't learn English?"

113

"That, and other things. Italians belong together anyway. Especially southern Italians."

I scratched dirt off my arm. "Let me get this straight. Immigrants who aren't Italian, they learn English?"

"Yeah. You should hear the big, dumb Swedes speaking English in the factories in Chatham Square."

"Dumb like a fox," I said. "The Italians are the dumb ones. It's better to learn English and get any job you want."

"What'd I tell you about being loyal?" said Gaetano. "Especially here, right now."

"Why especially here?" I asked.

"Because of the Irish. Shut up, okay?" Gaetano stopped. "See that big building across Prince Street? That's Saint Patrick's Cathedral."

The bells rang as we stood there. People came from the north and went through the central front door with the pointed arch over it. People came from behind us on Mulberry Street and went around to the side. Gaetano walked toward the side entrance.

"Why don't we go in the front door?" I asked.

"Because we're not Irish. Shut up. I mean it."

We went down to the basement. Everyone crowded onto benches. I stared straight ahead at the neck of the woman in front of me. She reached a hand up under her black mantilla and a curl tumbled down. Her hair wasn't as dark as Mamma's. But that curl made my face prickle with pins and needles. She tucked it back under. It fell again.

A priest came in. Everyone stood. For the next hour the priest spoke in an Italian that I could mostly understand and a Latin that I loved listening to. We stood and sat and kneeled and recited Latin. They passed around a basket. People put in coins. Not Gaetano.

The priest read a part of the Bible about Saint Paul working hard. Then he talked about the virtue of persisting against the odds. He talked about the opportunities that lay within reach for hard workers. He said Italians could never be faulted for not working hard. The people murmured agreement. He said the possibilities were endless for us—for every last one of us. I thought of Uncle Aurelio and his lectures on *le possibilità,* Uncle Aurelio, who would be aghast to see me at a Catholic mass. My whole family would. I was.

I stood up to leave, but Gaetano yanked me back into my seat. "Stay still," he hissed. "The gospel is the most important part."

I looked at my hands and tried to close my ears to what was going on outside my head. It was my body in this church, not my heart and soul.

Afterward, I asked Gaetano, "Why go to this church if the Irish make you sit in the basement? Aren't there Italian churches?"

"Sure there are. But they're outside Five Points. Here there're only Irish churches—the Most Precious Blood Church and the Church of the Transfiguration and this one—Saint Patrick's. But Italians have to sit in the basement at the other churches, too. And the Transfiguration is on Mott Street; I hate Mott Street. Anyway, it's better than it used to be—they used to forbid the priests from using Italian."

He pulled me into a building a block away. Adults

drank coffee and ate pastries. Kids ran around knocking into things. Gaetano stuffed a pastry in his mouth and filled a cup with coffee. I did the same. I didn't usually like coffee, but it was delicious at that moment. I hadn't had anything to eat since the ice cream Saturday afternoon.

"I've seen you here before," said a woman in an Italian dialect as she approached Gaetano. "But without your little brother. Where's your mother?"

"She's sick," said Gaetano, speaking her dialect—just like he'd spoken the ice cream vendor's Genovese the day before.

"That's too bad." She looked doubtful. "What's her name?"

Gaetano backed toward the door.

"Don't run off," said the woman. She picked up two more pastries and handed us each one. "If your family joins, then when someone gets sick, we'll help out. And when someone dies, we'll pay the funeral costs. Tell your mother that."

"I will," said Gaetano.

"Or, better, let me tell her." A little girl yanked on the woman's skirt. The woman picked her up without turning her eyes from us. "Where do you live?" One hand caressed the little girl's head. Mamma used to do that to me all the time. "I can bring your mother soup," said the woman, her hand on the child's cheek.

"We have to go." Gaetano put down his cup and took my hand. "We're late."

"See you next week," said the woman.

Gaetano pulled me outside and we ate our pastries. "Next week I'll go to a different one."

"A different what?" I asked, forcing away the picture of the woman's hand on the child's cheek. "Are there always parties after church?"

"It's not a party—it's a meeting of a mutual aid society. There are lots of them around here. Don't they have them in the Bronx?"

I shrugged. "What dialect were you talking with her?"

"Milanese. It's from the north of Italy."

"Do you speak every Italian dialect?" I asked.

"Nah. Only the useful ones. To tell the truth, I hardly speak Milanese at all. Just enough to keep out of trouble for sneaking in."

"Why don't you go to a mutual aid society for people from Napoli?"

Gaetano laughed. "There aren't any. It costs fifty cents a month to be a member. None of the southern Italians can afford that. And the northerners wouldn't let us join theirs anyway, even if we had the money."

"Why not?"

"They look down on us. And we don't care. Who needs them? Look. It's like this, Dom. You're Napoletano. I'm Napoletano. We're our own group. We stick together. But the next best guy is someone from the south—except for Sicilia. Don't ever trust a Siciliano. But the Calabresi aren't too bad. There's lots of them on Mulberry Street. And the ones from Basilicata—they're dirt poor and they know nothing, but they're okay. And then, after that, there's northern Italians. The Piemontesi and Lombardi. They live west of Broadway."

"Then who?"

"No one. After the Italians, there's no one you can trust."

"What else do these societies do beside help with funerals and take care of the sick?"

"Sometimes they get jobs for people. And if they can't find anything in New York, they'll pay your fare to the coal mines in Pennsylvania or West Virginia. Or, if you want to go farther, Colorado, or Wyoming, or Montana. But then you have to work with Slavs and Welshmen. Still, the mines will always hire Italians first."

Tonino had a job in a coal mine. He must be off in one of those places. "That's what you should do when you're older, Gaetano, start a mutual aid society for southern Italians, not some stupid bank."

"People who run mutual aid societies don't get rich. Bankers get rich."

Everything he said came out like the gospel of that priest—like a truth no one could argue with. "How do you know everything, Gaetano?"

"I pay attention."

"No one pays attention that well," I said.

He grinned. "They would if they got paid for it."

"You get paid for paying attention?"

"I see something someone would want to know—I hear something someone would want to know—and I sell the information." Gaetano sat down on the steps of a building and stretched his legs in front of him, crossed at the ankles. He leaned his elbows back on a higher step.

"How can you figure out what someone would want to know?"

"People need information. All kinds of information. They pay me for the craziest things. You wouldn't believe it. And don't get any ideas about sticking around here and

118

stealing my job. You'd never survive. You don't understand anything you see."

"Sticking around here is the last thing I want to do." I sat beside him. Gaetano really did understand everything he saw. People wouldn't pay him for information if he couldn't be trusted. "Want another job, Gaetano?"

"Who's offering? You? You've got nothing to pay with."

It killed me to say it—but what else did I have? "My shoes."

Gaetano sat up. "What's the job?"

"Get me onto the ship that's down at the wharves. The *Bolivia*."

"You want to go on a ship? Where?"

"Napoli."

Gaetano stared at me. Then he gasped. "You're not from the Bronx at all. You're fresh off the boat, aren't you? You're really lost." He slapped one fist into the other palm. "I should have known it."

"Why? How could you have known?"

He flushed. "If you had a mother, she'd have come storming down here by now." His temples pulsed. His jaw tightened.

"Is your mother really sick, like you told that woman?"

"That's none of your business."

"Do you have a mother?" I asked.

"Shut up. I mean it. Don't ever ask about my family."

I raised my hands in surrender, to calm him down. Then I leaned toward him. "Get me onto that ship and these shoes are yours."

"I don't go down to the wharves. You know that." Gaetano shook his head at me now. "You're alone. You don't even have a *padrone*. Now I get it. The way you act so much older than you are. That's all it takes—a few days alone, and you grow up just like that. What else could you do? I've seen it before. Kids like you, acting so big."

"You don't have to talk to anyone in English out there," I said. "Just come with me to the wharves—come and listen and watch. Figure out a way to get me on the ship. Please. I want to go home."

Gaetano looked away. I knew by now that that was what he did when he was trying to make up his mind. I squeezed my hands together.

He turned back to me. "I'm not promising a thing. But I'll see what I can find out. When's this ship sailing?"

"I don't know, but it's got to be soon."

"Meet you back here at suppertime." He got up and walked down Mulberry. "And don't follow me," he called over his shoulder.

So I went the other way, up Mulberry. No one talked to me. No one looked at me.

Mulberry ran into another street at an angle. If I kept going in the same general direction, there was no way I could get lost. The only thing I needed to know was where to angle off on the way back. I counted the number of streets I crossed. At the fifth corner, my street angled again. Well, okay, I could keep track of that. At the fifth corner, this street angled, too. That was easy to remember—five and five. I was at the edge of a park.

The street sign said PARK, with the little letters *A-V-E* in the upper right corner. I knew *park*. It was the one word of English I could read. And suddenly I made the connection—the Italian word *parco* and the English word *park*—they must mean the same thing. English wasn't such a hard language, after all.

Could this possibly be the same Park Street that ran into Chatham Square? Just in case it wasn't, I counted blocks again. I walked along looking around at the tall buildings, the passing carriages, the people. Stores were closed and shuttered, but I looked at the carvings in the stone over doorways and the huge, feathered hats that the ladies wore. Most of the women held on to the arm of a man. One woman strode by me with a frilly white blouse and a skirt with a wide waistband. Two rows of buttons ran down the front of her blouse. She wasn't pretty, but she caught the eye. Mamma would have been beautiful in those clothes.

I lost count of the blocks somewhere after twenty, because I looked up and my breath was taken away. A giant building loomed ahead. There were three levels of windows. I walked along one side counting the cupolas. Behind the building was a large train shed. Oh, it was a railway station.

I went inside. Men in white straw hats with black bands around the center and broad brims stood in groups. Some carried canes, though they weren't old. They wore ties and vests under their jackets and spoke English.

But then I saw men with curly black hair and mustaches and bow ties. They spoke Napoletano and they bought tickets to Bronxville. Eight cents for a twenty-minute ride. They complained about the high fare, but that was what it cost to visit the relatives on Sunday.

I went out to the train platforms. A gleaming steam engine pulled in. I watched people and trains for hours. When I got too hungry to stay still, I left, passing an area

121

where they kept baggage. A penny to check your belongings overnight.

A penny for this, a penny for that. Life in New York was measured out in pennies.

It was hours yet till suppertime. So I let myself wander. After all, I could say "park" and anyone could point me back to the right road.

Within a couple of blocks I wound up on a broad street. I followed it a long way and came to the countryside. Look at that. Manhattan wasn't such a big place after all. I'd walked the whole length of it. Where there was country, there were farms—and where there were farms, there was food.

A family sprawled on tablecloths spread out on the grass, finishing a meal. The smell of strange spices hung in the air. Fancy food. And these people looked fancy—not at all like farmers. They wore their Sunday best.

I hid behind a tree and watched. A few children took handfuls of leftovers and ran toward a pond. Three huge waterbirds, white things with long necks, swam at the edge. They looked toward the children expectantly. One of them got out of the water and waddled up.

The children screamed and laughed and threw food at the birds. Perfectly good food.

I ran out and grabbed a handful. It looked like a pastry with something green in the middle. Spinach?

Honk! A big bird charged me, flapping giant wings. *Honk honk honk!* I clutched the food and ran. The bird ran faster. It bit the back of my pant leg, its huge bill clamping onto my flesh. I threw the pastry at it. The bird let go and

122

swallowed it whole, then honked at me. But I was already running again. The bird went back to the water.

I watched from a safe distance. How could such beautiful birds be so nasty? I was sure they weren't as hungry as I was. They looked sleek and clean.

I was so dirty. And thirsty. That water looked pretty good. I circled the pond and went down to its edge farther up, far from the dangerous birds.

I drank and washed my face. Then I rolled up my pant legs and waded in. The bird had left two red marks on the back of my calf, but the skin wasn't broken.

My hair was clumped with filth, so I leaned forward and dunked my head and rubbed at my hair. It felt so good.

When I turned, a woman stood on the shore. She was from the family whose children had fed those birds. She waved and put a piece of paper on the ground with food on it. Then she walked away.

I waded out and grabbed the paper. I wolfed down a pastry: spinach with a sour white cheese. And there was eggplant with beef and a sauce. The sauce was white—oh, no. I licked it. It didn't taste like milk or cheese, so maybe it was white from flour. If that was so, the dish was kosher—no mixing of milk and meat. Should I risk it?

Chi nun risica nun roseca—He who doesn't risk, doesn't gain. One of Nonna's proverbs. But I'd never heard her say it about risking breaking kosher laws. Still . . .

I nibbled. It was good. I ate all of it. Then there was a corner of sweet pastry with nuts and honey. What a feast. Not Italian food, but good food.

I wandered off to view the farms I expected to find past

the next set of trees. There were only more trees, though, and more paths with more people. I came upon a throng of people. Out for a Sunday stroll in the sun. And here was a wide set of stairs with a big fountain and another pond. People took rides on little boats with awning tops. This wasn't the countryside at all. It was a colossal park. The atmosphere was like that at a saint festival; everyone was happy and talking and calling to their children. The women had parasols with lace at the edges. In Napoli rich women held them to keep the sun off their faces.

I could pick out English easily. But there were many other languages, too.

Bicyclists went past with white caps and numbers on their shirts. On another path, people rode by on horseback. How big was this park, anyway?

I went in a straight line until I hit a road on one side. Then I went in a straight line in the opposite direction until I hit a road on the other side. It was as far across this park as it was from my home in Napoli to the bottom of Via Toledo.

Now I walked along one edge to find out how long the park was north to south. But it was getting late and people were leaving, so I had to start back. I walked and walked and walked. It took more than an hour to get to the south end of the park. I ran. Stupid me. Gaetano would be waiting on the steps by now.

The street was empty of walkers and only the occasional carriage passed. I tried to flag one down. The driver yelled at me and sped up. The next one did the same.

I ran faster. I heard a train to my left. Good, that was where the depot was supposed to be. I ran a long way.

Then I turned and went two streets over. The streetlamps were lit now, and the sign said PARK. Everything was exactly how it was supposed to be, except that I was late. I couldn't run anymore. I was out of breath. And I got spooked by every shadow. The buildings were too tall here. Who knew what could jump out from between them, or fall from a window high up?

I walked in the street, at the edge so carriages wouldn't hit me. Finally, I came to the medium-size park and I ran by the steps of Saint Patrick's Cathedral to the mutual aid society.

It was night by now; what a fool I'd been to stay in the park so long.

No Gaetano.

I went to my barrel and slept.

CHAPTER FOURTEEN

Sandwiches

On Monday the alley came alive with loud bangs long before dawn. I leapt out of my barrel and ran to the next street before I dared to look back. It was street cleaners, lugging trash out to a wagon and shouting in English. They took away the dead dog, and with it the stench that meant no one would come near my barrel.

Who cared, anyway? I was leaving on the *Bolivia* soon. Maybe that day.

Girls who were almost young ladies walked along the block toward me, arm in arm. They wore black skirts down to their ankles and white aprons and blouses with black bows at the neck. They had on black boots. I flattened myself against the wall as they passed, talking of someone named Maria Luisa, who had the good fortune to be getting married. She

wouldn't have to work anymore. Their voices were as-
toundingly loud.

I looked around. No Gaetano. I might as well head for
the wharf.

I got there in record time, running so hard I had to
bend to wheeze on the last corner.

The *Bolivia* was gone.

Noooo. I ran into the nearest cafe. "What happened to
the ship?" I asked.

The man making coffee said something in English.

"*Bolivia*," I said. "*Bolivia.*" I pointed to the wharf.

The man said something else in English, then went and
served his customers.

This wasn't possible.

A policeman passed the window. I ran outside to him.
"*Bolivia*," I said.

He looked down at me with fat, ruddy cheeks and said
something in English.

I pointed to where the ship had been. "*Bolivia.*"

The policeman shooed me away.

It couldn't have left. It must have just moved to another
dock. Someone had to know.

I looked around for the Italian bricklayers. But the
sidewalk in front of the shop was perfect; they'd finished
the job. Well, maybe they'd be back. I leaned against the
shop window and sank to my bottom, my knees pressed
against my chest.

The shopkeeper showed up to unlock.

"*Bolivia?*" I said.

He got out a broom and shook it at me.

I ran along the waterfront. I ran and ran. But who was

I kidding? If there was a ship docked anywhere along here, everyone could have seen it from far away.

The *Bolivia* was gone.

I kept running, without thinking, back and forth along the wharf, back and forth, back and forth. Tears blurred my vision.

Traffic had picked up; the day was really started. Another day here. In New York, in America, an ocean away from home.

I stopped and leaned my forehead against a pole and waited for my eyes to clear. Then I walked back up the road.

"Who died?" It was Tin Pan Alley, standing on his corner, the tin cup at his feet, the triangle in his hand.

"The ship left. The *Bolivia*. I was supposed to go on it. But it left without me."

"That's bad." He tapped his triangle and whistled the tune about the bicycle built for two.

I stood there, too sad to move.

Tin Pan Alley reached in his pocket and took out a small brown rock. He threw it on the sidewalk. It split into shards. He scooped some back into his pocket and he put the rest in my hand.

I looked at them.

"Rock candy," he said. "An old Chinese man gave it to me."

I looked at it. "I can't take that. I bet you almost never get candy."

"How often do you get ice cream? You're not the only one who can share." He tapped his triangle again. "I have to work hard now. The early crowd is good on Monday. Come back in a couple of hours."

"Why?" I said.

"You got something better to do?" He whistled.

I put my hands in my pockets and watched the people go by. The ship had left. Without me. But . . . another had to be coming soon. This was a delay—that was all. The job now was to get ready for the next ship. That was what Uncle Aurelio would have said.

I sucked on the rock candy. The sweetness made my mouth water—and now all I wanted was real food. I went back to the produce vendor on Mulberry Street, who was polishing fruit with a towel and arranging it in piles.

"Tomatoes should go in front," I said.

He turned around. "So you're back."

"They'll catch the eye better. Red does that. Then the green zucchini should go at the back. And the onions can stay in the baskets on the ground in front of the table. All they really need is for the ones on top to be brushed off a little."

"All right, all right, you've convinced me. Go to work."

"But I need three oranges today."

"Oranges get trucked up from Florida, in the south. They don't grow around here. It's not like the south of Italy. They cost."

"I'll work as long as it takes to earn them. I'm good at sweeping, too."

He threw his towel over his shoulder. "Arrange the produce. Then we'll talk."

I worked for an hour. I put everything in its perfect place.

"Beautiful," the vendor said. "What's your name, kid?"

"Dom."

"I'm Grandinetti. Francesco Grandinetti. Can I trust you, Dom?"

"Yes."

"Let's find out. Here's a penny. Go to the corner and pick me up an Italian paper."

"Do they speak Italian at the newsstand?"

"Yes."

I bought the newspaper. Then I ran back to Grandinetti's.

He spread out the paper on the weighing counter inside and pointed. "What can you make of that?"

The paper was full of drawings of people with words printed in little clouds over their heads. One guy was saying he needed to use the bathroom. The other was talking about money. It didn't make much sense to me. I glanced up at Grandinetti.

"Don't worry about the words," he said. "You don't have to be able to read to get it."

"I can read," I said.

He smiled like he didn't believe me. "Most people lie and say they can read. That's why there's lots of illustrations. See? I got a customer. You look at the paper."

I turned the page. These illustrations were of people working in factories. A man yelled at them and brandished a whip. The people were small and scrawny and dark-skinned. The boss was tall and fat and light-skinned.

Grandinetti came back in and weighed carrots and lettuce and tomatoes and onions for a woman in a bright flowered dress. Her face was powdered so white she looked

130

sick. She watched every move he made, as though afraid he'd cheat her. She left in a haze of strong perfume.

"She watched you weigh everything," I said.

"She's a widow." Grandinetti tsked. "She's got it as hard as anyone. Most people would cheat her if they could."

"Not you."

"No. But you don't know me well enough to say that yet. Did you read the paper?"

I pointed. "Are the workers Italian?"

"Yes."

"And is the boss Irish?"

Grandinetti smiled. "You've got it all figured out."

"At church yesterday, the Italians went into the basement, while the Irish went upstairs."

"The church belonged to the Irish first. This used to be their neighborhood."

"Doesn't a church belong to whoever goes to it?" I asked.

"Spoken like an Italian, my boy. Look, the Irish fill the offering basket with money. They pay for the church. The Italians have close to nothing to give, but even if they had it, they wouldn't pay the same way. To us, the priest is like a friend. We offer him produce or a pie. We have him over to supper. So . . . that's how it is . . . the Irish get the upstairs."

"And they get all the jobs. So why stay here? Why not get on the next ship back to Italy?"

"Is that what your father says? Listen here, Dom. Lots of us had it rough at first. America's not perfect, God knows. In Calabria I farmed—and after living an outdoor life like that, being in the city is like being in a cage.

131

Sometimes I can hardly stand it. But in Italy my family was always struggling. Here, we're doing better."

I tapped the illustration. "That's 'cause you're not working in a factory."

"In Italy workers get paid whenever the boss feels like it—here they get paid every week. In Italy men have to work till the job's finished, no matter how long it takes— here they work till quitting time. It's better here. Your father will get used to it. An Irish boss who pays on time is better than an Italian boss who doesn't." He waved to someone out on the sidewalk. "A customer. There's a bushel of new potatoes in the storeroom. Go through them and set the biggest ones on the floor."

I had sorted the potatoes by the time Grandinetti finished with his customer. He put the small potatoes aside and wrapped the big ones in newspaper. "The Cassone family lives on Mott, at the corner of Canal Street, left-hand side. There's a high tenement there. They're two flights up. Bring these to them, okay?"

"Yes, sir."

He handed me three oranges. "Valencias. Juicy. See you tomorrow?"

"Yes, sir."

I put an orange in each pocket and kept the third in my hand.

Sure enough, Gaetano was by my side within a half block, and his eyes went immediately to the orange in my hand.

"The ship's gone," I said.

"I know. It left last night."

I knew he'd know. "I'm a mook. I took a walk way up by this huge railway station. . . ."

"Grand Central Depot? You saw Grand Central Depot? What's it like?"

"It's huge. And then I went to a giant park with ponds and people on boats. . . ."

"Central Park. I can't believe you went all the way to Central Park. Did you see the swans? Did you play in the fountain?"

"And by the time I got back here it was night. I'm the biggest mook there is."

"You're not a mook," said Gaetano.

"You don't have to be nice to me," I said. "I'm going to give you this orange anyway. You earned it by finding out how to get me on the *Bolivia,* whether I ruined everything or not."

"I couldn't get you on that ship. The security is tight. Everyone told me it's impossible. The only way on that ship is with a ticket. So it doesn't matter whether you were late last night or not. Keep the orange."

"It's for you." I handed it to him. He tried to hand it back. "Eat it," I said. "We're friends."

"Friends." He tossed the orange from hand to hand. "This is just 'cause we're friends?"

I smiled. "Well, it's for helping me get on the next ship, too."

"Oh. Look," said Gaetano softly. "There's something else."

"What?"

"Maybe with a lot of bribing you could have gotten on

that ship without a ticket—or if not that ship, another one. I don't know. It's not likely."

"What do you mean, it's not likely? Another ship will be different," I said. "They can't all be so hard."

"I don't know, Dom. Maybe bribing would work. Only . . ."

"Only what?"

"The guy I talked to said you needed documents to get on a ship—any ship—because if you get caught, the crew member gets in trouble. And the penalty for letting some-one sneak on is worse if the stowaway doesn't have documents."

I practically laughed in relief. "I've got documents."

"No, you don't."

I reached into my pocket. But the folded papers the translator on Ellis Island had given me were gone. I stopped and stared at Gaetano. He looked down. His temples pulsed. "You knew they were gone. You stole them!"

"Don't talk so loud." Gaetano took me by the arm.

I pulled free. "Give them back."

"I can't."

"Give them back!" I shouted.

"I sold them."

"Then just go unsell them! Right now!"

"Be quiet, will you?" Gaetano looked around, then took a step toward me. "I can't," he said in a loud whisper. "I sold them Saturday. I tried to get them back yesterday, but the guy had already sold them to someone else."

"No. That's not possible."

Gaetano bounced the orange against his chest and stared at the ground.

I couldn't believe what an idiot I was. Here I'd been worried about guarding my shoes, when those papers were so much more important, and I hadn't even checked on them since Friday night. If I had checked on Saturday, I would have guessed that Gaetano had taken them. I could have gone to him and made him get them back before the other guy sold them. What a brainless mook. I hadn't even noticed that they were gone when I washed off in the park. Or when I put the oranges in my pockets. I should have, I should have, I should have. I stamped my feet and turned in a circle.

Now I couldn't get on any ship. Ever. "You're a thief. You're a dirty thief after all." I ran along the sidewalk, clutching the package with the potatoes.

Gaetano ran beside me.

I wanted to hurl the potatoes at him—knock him into the street. Maybe a carriage would run him over. I turned and swung the package hard.

Gaetano pinned me against a wall.

"Help!" I screamed. "Thief!"

"Shut up a second." He panted in my face. "Look, I thought you were some rich kid from the Bronx. I didn't even know what the papers were. Not till the guy who bought them told me. I'd never seen documents before. They're hard to come by. I didn't know you were alone. I wouldn't have done it otherwise. I swear."

"Thief."

"We weren't friends yet."

"We aren't friends."

"Yes, we are," said Gaetano.

"You don't know what a friend is."

135

Gaetano jerked his head back as though I'd punched him. He put the orange in my free hand. "I didn't have to tell you," he said. "I didn't have to say anything about the documents. You'd have thought you lost them in that barrel you sleep in every night." He turned and walked off slowly.

I wanted to throw the orange at his head. He couldn't make me feel sorry for what I'd said just because he'd told the truth. And because he knew where I slept and he hadn't stolen my shoes. He was the one who had done something rotten, not me. And I was the one who was stuck here. "Give me the money you got from selling them," I called.

Gaetano stopped and stood there, his back to me.

I had no choice but to catch up.

"I spent it." He turned to face me. "On a steak lunch."

"So I'm stuck here now. I'm stuck here and it's your fault."

Gaetano spread his hands, palms up. His eyes were solemn. "I'll let people know I want documents. Maybe someone will sell me some soon."

"They're hard to come by," I said. "Guess who told me?"

Gaetano's temples pulsed. "I'm your friend. I'll never do anything bad to you again."

What was left for him to do to me? Nothing would seem bad in comparison. All at once, I was too tired to argue.

He fell into step beside me. "Look."

I dragged my feet. I wasn't even hungry anymore.

He cleared his throat. "I'm sorry, Dom."

His apology caught me. I didn't want it to. I wanted to hate him. It wasn't fair, what he had done.

136

But what was?

Napoletano boys didn't apologize. That sorry cost Gaetano. He wanted my friendship a lot.

How come? What was his story, anyway? The other day he'd said he stayed alone, but he'd told me not to ask where he slept. And later, when I wondered if he had a mother, he'd told me never to ask about his family. He'd said it as though it was a sacred rule: don't ask. How did he get here? What happened to his parents? Why didn't he have a *padrone*, at least? Don't ask, don't ask.

I stopped and looked around. I was either with Gaetano or totally alone. "Do you really think you could buy more documents?"

"I can try," said Gaetano. "It'd probably cost a lot."

At least he was telling the truth now. I tossed him the orange. He caught it.

We walked up the street in silence.

When we got to the corner of Mott, Gaetano asked, "Where are you going? I hate this street."

"Then don't come. I didn't ask you to."

"Wherever you're going, I'm going," said Gaetano. "You're only nine."

"How'd you find that out? From my documents? Don't do me any favors. I'm fine on my own."

"Then I'm coming because we're friends."

"Suit yourself," I said.

We turned onto Mott Street.

"You shouldn't go here," said Gaetano. "The Chinese have been moving in."

"What's wrong with the Chinese?"

"They're tricky. You should see. They get jobs all over

the place rolling cigars. I've heard they make as much as twenty-five dollars a week. An Italian laborer gets a dollar a day. The lowest of anyone."

"What do you mean, the lowest of anyone?"

"Whites get a dollar and twenty-five cents a day. Negroes get a dollar and fifteen cents a day. Italians get a dollar."

"For the same work?"

"Yeah."

"What do the Chinese get for a day's labor?"

"No one hires them for day work. They're too skinny. But Italians are strong and still they get paid bad. And if there's any difference in the types of jobs, Italians are allowed only at the worst ones. They can't collect the piles of garbage, they can only shovel it off barges into the sea."

"So you're jealous of the Chinese."

"I'm not jealous," said Gaetano. "That's ridiculous. You should hear the Chinese talk English. They're horrible. Everyone makes fun of them."

"Yeah, you're jealous," I said. "Here we are." We went into the tenement and up two flights. There were three doors. "Which one do I knock on?"

"Who are you looking for?"

"The Cassone family."

A little girl was coming down the stairs. She pointed. "At the front."

"I could have told you," said Gaetano. "They hang out the window at night and watch the action on Canal Street. I told you. I know all of Five Points."

I knocked.

The door opened. A woman with puffy lips and white

hair pulled back tight into a bun looked at us in a daze. A younger man gently moved her aside. He glared. "What do you want?" His breath was rancid.

I handed him the potatoes. "Grandinetti told me to bring you these."

The old woman took the package from the man. "I'll make potato and fried egg sandwiches for breakfast," she said. "Your favorite."

The man said, "Thanks," and shut the door.

We went downstairs. The smell of potatoes sizzling in oil already wafted past our noses. And rosemary. And pepper. It was heavenly. Gaetano rolled that orange in his hands. I bet he hadn't had any breakfast, either.

But he'd had a steak lunch two days before. On me.

Still, hunger came every day.

"Go ahead and eat the orange," I said. "I've got two more. One for me and one for Tin Pan Alley. I'm going to the corner where he works." I looked at him with a dare in my eyes. "Come if you want."

"Nah, I'll see you later."

"What about all that stuff you said before—all that stuff about coming because you're my friend?"

"You know the way," said Gaetano. "Besides, I don't like that mook."

"You're the mook, you know that, Gaetano?"

"Hey, I said I was sorry about the documents."

"That's not what I'm talking about. You speak every dialect of Italian, and then you're afraid of English. So you live your whole life in just these few blocks. I've seen more of this city than you have. What a stupid way to live. You're the biggest rabbit I've ever known."

139

"I'm no rabbit. I'm afraid of nothing."

"You're afraid to go with me to see Tin Pan Alley."

"No, I'm not."

"Prove it."

We walked fast all the way to Tin Pan Alley's corner, eating our oranges.

"Hey," I said, and handed Tin Pan Alley the orange.

"What's this?" he said.

"What do you think?" I said. "Eat it."

"Are you kidding?"

"I can't believe it's so hard to give away oranges. What's with you two?"

"Don't throw me in the same category as this mook," said Gaetano. "I had a reason for not taking mine. He's just dumb."

"I have a reason," said Tin Pan Alley. "If this is really mine, I'm selling it. This is Wall Street. The people who work down here don't know the value of money. They get big salaries. I can get five cents for this orange. You don't believe me, but it's true. The big guys spend as much as fifty cents for a sandwich here, and it's small."

"Fifty cents? That's a fortune," said Gaetano. "How do you know?"

"I heard someone say it."

"In English?" asked Gaetano. "Maybe you didn't understand right."

Tin Pan Alley smirked. "I understood."

"It's not your orange," I said. I took it back.

Tin Pan Alley didn't look surprised. "So what," he said, and turned his back to me. He wasn't going to fight. I wanted to shake him. I knew how to fight back better than him when I was five years old.

I peeled the orange and broke it into sections. Then I walked around to the front of him. "You can't sell it now. So you might as well eat it."

"That was dumb," said Tin Pan Alley. But even as he spoke, his hand reached out. He put an orange section in his mouth. His eyelids half closed as he chewed.

So far that day I'd eaten only rock candy and one orange. I couldn't risk looking at the orange sections in my hand, or I might gobble them up.

Tin Pan Alley smiled. "Now and then dumb makes sense." He ate another section. "Five cents lost. But, oh . . ." He ate another and another.

"Five cents is nothing compared to fifty," I said.

"Fifty?" Tin Pan Alley's eyes sharpened. His cheeks pinched, as though he was sure I was about to pull a fast one on him.

"You're going to be eating a lot of oranges from now on." I put the rest of the orange in his hand.

"What are you talking about?"

"I've got an idea." And it was a beauty, all right. I could hear Mamma in my head, telling me to be my own boss. "Come on, Gaetano, hurry."

Gaetano had been watching me this whole time as though he couldn't figure me out. But now he flinched to attention. "Why?"

I was already racing toward Five Points. "Can you get your hands on some clean paper?"

"What for?"

141

"That brown paper the ice cream man uses—that would do."

"Yeah. I can get some. What for?"

"And can you get a knife?"

"A knife? Whoa. Tell me what for or I don't want any part of it."

"Forget the knife. I bet Grandinetti has a knife I can use. Just get the paper."

By this time, we were at the corner of Park Street. Gaetano grabbed my arm. "What's going on?"

"I'm going to make money, Gaetano. Lots. And Tin Pan Alley is going to help me. You can be part of it, unless you're too much of a rabbit."

"You think I'm stupid enough to do something just because you call me names?" he said. "I do what I want to do. And I don't hurt anyone. No knives."

"We won't hurt a soul. I'm going to earn enough money for a ticket home and new documents. You want something, that's for sure. You're always hungry. Except when you're eating steak. So are you in?"

"All I have to do is get brown paper?"

"Yeah. Four big pieces."

"What about that knife?" he said.

"Just get the paper and meet me at Grandinetti's."

"Where?"

"The produce store. And if I'm not there, wait for me, 'cause I'll be coming."

I ran to Grandinetti's. He was standing behind the weighing counter, reading the paper. "Please," I said.

Grandinetti looked over the edge of the paper at me. "Please what?"

The words burst out of me. "I need to borrow twenty-five cents. Only for a couple of hours."

"I'm not a bank." He clapped his hands together in front of his chest as though he was praying and shook them at me. "Small as you are, you're a good worker. You keep it up and I'll be square with you. But I'm no chump."

"Here." I took off my shoes. "You can keep them if I don't pay you back by the end of the day."

Grandinetti frowned. "Your folks will be angry if you come home without your shoes."

"I'll have my shoes at the end of the day—and you'll have your twenty-five cents. Please."

"I don't want to face your angry father."

"I don't have a father."

Grandinetti blinked. "Your shoes are worth more than twenty-five cents—but twenty-five cents is all I'll lend you."

"That's all I'm asking for."

"All right."

"And do you have a knife I can use?"

"What's this all about?"

"I'm just going to cut a sandwich with it."

"Bring the sandwich in here," he said. "I'll cut it."

I took the twenty-five cents and ran barefoot to Luigi Pierano's store on Park Street. I bought a long sandwich stuffed with salami and provolone and hot peppers and onions and tomatoes and lettuce, nodding my head yes to everything he offered.

At Grandinetti's, Gaetano was waiting with the brown paper.

Grandinetti shook his head. "Exactly how do you expect to get your shoes back?"

"I'll bring you money, I swear. Just cut the sandwich into four equal sections. Please."

"His shoes, for a picnic," said Grandinetti under his breath as he cut the sandwich.

Gaetano and I wrapped the four pieces. Then we ran back to Wall Street. We didn't have to talk; Gaetano knew what was up.

"Here." I held out the cut sandwiches to Tin Pan Alley. "Sell them. Fifty cents."

"Sandwiches?" He looked around. "I'm not a vendor. I just make music."

"You were going to sell the orange," said Gaetano.

"One orange. That's easy. But I can't sell four sandwiches. Who would buy them from me? People have to trust food vendors."

"Try," I said.

One side of Tin Pan Alley's mouth rose nervously. He held out a sandwich to a passing man. "Sandwich?" he said in English.

The man looked at the sandwich. Then he looked at me, standing behind Tin Pan Alley with three more sandwiches. I smiled at him and tried to look trustworthy. He looked at Gaetano. Gaetano smiled at him. He said something in English to Tin Pan Alley.

"Chicken," said Tin Pan Alley in English.

The man said something else in English. Then he handed Tin Pan Alley a coin, took the sandwich, and walked away.

"A quarter," said Gaetano.

"How much is a quarter worth?" I asked.

"Twenty-five cents."

"That's only half of fifty." I pointed at Tin Pan Alley. "You said they'd pay fifty cents for a sandwich."

"So what," said Tin Pan Alley. "I didn't tell the guy the price. That's just what he gave me. Don't get mad."

"Mad?" Gaetano grinned. "You're both mooks. A quarter! That crazy man just paid a whole quarter for a sandwich. Tin Pan Alley, you were right; the people here have no sense of the value of money. They'll pay anything, and we've still got three more sandwiches to sell." He slapped Tin Pan Alley on the back. "It worked! Dom's crazy plan worked!"

It did. It worked. Gaetano saw things right. I grinned at Tin Pan Alley, too. "What does *chicken* mean?"

"It's the English word for *pollo*. He asked what was in the sandwich."

"But there's no chicken in the sandwich," I said.

"It was the only English word for meat I could think of. I hope the guy likes salami."

CHAPTER FIFTEEN

Money

The next three sandwiches were harder to sell. People walked by without giving us a look. But then a group of young men dressed in identical suits and ties came up. They took all three and gave Tin Pan Alley a handful of coins.

Tin Pan Alley counted. "Nine nickels."

"What's a nickel worth?" I asked.

"Five cents."

"That's only forty-five cents." I looked around for the men. They were just going through the door of a building. I ran. Spun. And fell.

Gaetano had hooked my elbow with such force that I'd been knocked off my feet. "Forget it. You can't go in there."

"They cheated us."

"And we'll get cheated again." Gaetano put his fists on his hips. "That's how it works."

"Look at it this way," said Tin Pan Alley. "We're forty-five cents ahead. Forty-five cents!"

"For once the mook is right." Gaetano grinned. "Forty-five whole cents."

And it wasn't even lunchtime yet. All right, this was okay.

Gaetano and I went back to Five Points, me racing ahead straight to Grandinetti's. I put the quarter on the counter under his nose.

"That was quick." Grandinetti reached under the counter and took out my shoes. He raised his brows in question.

I didn't want to explain. Not yet. There was still a lot to figure out. It felt like a dream, it was going so fast. If everything went the way I wanted it to, I'd be home in Napoli in no time.

So I sat on the floor and brushed off my feet and just smiled up at Grandinetti. Then I put on my shoes and rubbed them shiny with my thumbs. Gaetano waited for me out on the street. He was still grinning. I waved to him through the open door.

When I stood, I reached out to shake Grandinetti's hand.

He gave a crooked smile and hesitated. But he shook firmly.

"Keep your knife ready," I said. "We'll be right back."

"I'm not going anywhere."

The instant I stepped out the door, Gaetano grabbed me by the sleeve and pulled me down the block. "Look, I've got this all worked out. Give me five cents."

"No," I said. "Let's keep buying as many long sandwiches as we have money for. The more we sell, the more we make."

"If you don't give me five, what are we going to wrap the cut sandwiches in? No one will buy a sandwich that's been sitting in our bare hands. We need paper."

"Paper costs five cents?"

"No, you mook. I got the last four pieces for a penny. So that means the business owes me a penny. And with the other four pennies I'll buy sixteen more pieces. Sixteen, 'cause we have to look ahead."

His words rang in my head: *the business*. We had a business already. I gave Gaetano a nickel.

He headed for Baxter Street.

I made a beeline for Pierano's and bought another sandwich. Grandinetti cut it into four pieces. Gaetano and I wrapped the pieces in the new brown paper. But when we got to the fourth sandwich, Gaetano stopped. "Could you cut this one again?" he asked Grandinetti.

I knew immediately that he was thinking of our lunch. I almost objected. But hunger held my tongue.

Grandinetti nodded in approval. "Halves, huh?"

"Thirds," said Gaetano.

"Fourths," I said.

I wrapped the three parts of sandwich for Gaetano and Tin Pan Alley and me in a single sheet of brown paper and left the last part on the counter.

"What's this?" asked Grandinetti, surprised.

"Thank you for cutting the sandwiches," I said.

"You didn't have to do that."

When Gaetano and I were out on the street, Gaetano hissed, "He's right; you didn't have to do that."

"He helped us," I said.

"Yeah, but no one's going to see him eating. It's no advertisement for us."

Advertisement. Gaetano had a head for business. We found Tin Pan Alley back at his corner. I stood there beside him like a statue, holding the three wrapped sandwiches. Tin Pan Alley was the hawker, and when anyone would show a little interest, he'd point at Gaetano, who would take a big bite from one of the smaller pieces of sandwich that were for us, making loud *yum* noises. It worked; a man bought a sandwich. And for a whole quarter. Then it was Tin Pan Alley's turn to eat a small section of sandwich—but neither Gaetano nor I could hawk because we didn't speak English, so that didn't work so well. Still, we sold another sandwich. Only one to go.

Now it was my turn to eat that little section of sandwich. The sandwiches had meat and cheese mixed together. Plus, the meat was salami—probably made of pig. I picked out a piece of salami, but then I didn't know where to put it.

"What are you doing?" said Gaetano.

"I don't like salami," I said.

"Eat it anyway. When you mess up the sandwich like that, you make it look bad."

A potential customer was watching us.

"Make a game of it," said Tin Pan Alley. "Act like a dog, Gaetano."

"I'm no dog!"

"No, a dog's smarter than you," said Tin Pan Alley. He got on his knees and barked.

I fed him the salami. Then I took a bite of my piece of sandwich, careful to eat only cheese and lettuce.

The man bought the last wrapped sandwich.

Lunchtime was over. It had taken more than an hour to sell three sandwiches. But who cared? We had seventy-five cents to add to the fifteen already in my pocket.

"See you tomorrow," I said to Tin Pan Alley.

Gaetano and I headed back toward Five Points.

"Wait," called Tin Pan Alley. "Where's my share?"

"You got something to eat," said Gaetano. "Woof, woof. Remember?"

"No fair. The whole time we were selling, I wasn't making music. So no one put money in my cup. And lunch is one of my best times. What did you give up? Nothing."

"Are you saying my time's worth nothing?" Gaetano's hands balled into fists.

"The only thing I saw you do was eat," said Tin Pan Alley. "I'm the one who actually sold the sandwiches. Without me, you couldn't say a word. You need me."

Gaetano thrust his chin forward. "You need me, too, you little mook."

"Hold on," I said. "Let's put together what we have till the end of the week. The more long sandwiches we buy, the more small ones we sell. We'll make real money this way."

Gaetano put his face in mine. "I want my share now. That's what we agreed on."

I moved my face even closer to Gaetano's. "Lots and lots of money. And we still have twelve pieces of brown paper. We can start the day tomorrow with three long sandwiches." I cleared my throat. "One week, that's all I'm asking."

Gaetano looked away. When he looked back, he nodded. "One week."

"No," said Tin Pan Alley. "If I don't bring in eighty cents today, I'll get a beating."

I dropped ten cents in Tin Pan Alley's cup.

"I would have made double that."

"We only earned ninety cents. And we need seventy-five for the three sandwiches tomorrow morning. How about I give you fifteen?" I put another nickel in Tin Pan Alley's cup.

Tin Pan Alley just looked at it.

"Come on, mook." Gaetano picked salami from his teeth. "Money makes money. Beg harder this afternoon."

Tin Pan Alley glared at him.

"Oh, I forgot. You don't beg. Well, play your stupid triangle harder."

"He whistles, too," I said. "He whistles good."

"Come on," said Gaetano. "We're partners."

I remembered the welts on the boy with the harp in Chatham Square. Did it really matter whether we started the next day with two sandwiches instead of three?

"Get out of here," Tin Pan Alley spat. He turned his back and played the triangle.

"Wait," I said. "Here's another nickel. . . ."

"Go!" Tin Pan Alley was swaying back and forth, he played that triangle so hard.

Gaetano dragged me off. "Shut up. And open your stupid eyes."

I looked over my shoulder. A big man in a wide-brimmed hat stood near the lamppost with his arms crossed on his chest. His feet were spread far apart and his stomach pushed forward. His eyes were on Tin Pan Alley. Now he glanced at us.

I looked straight ahead and practically ran to keep up with Gaetano. "Is that . . . ?"

"His *padrone*. Of course."

Goose bumps went up my arms and neck. "How'd you know?"

"You can always tell a *padrone*."

"How?"

"From the stink."

We didn't slow down till we got to Chatham Square. "Is Tin Pan Alley in trouble?"

He looked away. "We'll find out tomorrow."

"He didn't do anything bad," I said.

"*Padroni* don't need a reason. Forget about it till tomorrow."

Tomorrow. Our business. "See you in the morning, right? Same deal?"

"Not exactly." Gaetano folded his arms across his chest. For a second he looked a little like the *padrone*. "We can improve."

"How?"

"Follow me and learn."

So we went to a paper mill. Inside, the clanking of the machines was so loud, I put my fingers in my ears. The workers didn't seem to be bothered by it, though. They hollered to one another above the din. Gaetano hollered to the manager; then the two of us went back out to the sidewalk and sat on the curb.

"For twenty-five cents we could buy a roll of paper long enough to wrap a thousand sandwiches at least," yelled Gaetano.

"Why are you shouting?" I yelled back.

Gaetano laughed. So did I. And I remembered those girls talking loud that morning as they walked past my alley. They probably worked in a noisy factory. The city must be full of near-deaf factory workers.

"You're the one who's good with numbers," said Gaetano. "But anyone can figure out that buying from the mill is cheaper than paying the ice cream man a penny for four sheets."

"I don't know," I said.

"What's to know?"

"Let's be careful. Spend just a little to start."

"And you're the one who wants to buy a boat ticket." Gaetano looked disgusted. "Besides, *chi poco spenne assai spenne*."

He who spends little winds up spending much more in the end—it had the sound of a proverb, one I hadn't heard before. But Gaetano couldn't win the argument just because he knew proverbs. "You really think we're going to have to sell a thousand sandwiches before I have enough money to get back home?"

"For a ticket and fake documents, you bet, 'cause we're going to share the money equally and we have to stay alive in the meantime."

"But if we spend twenty-five cents now," I said, "that's four fewer sandwiches we can sell tomorrow."

"You're talking like a mook again. Think about it. Think about how many sandwiches we can sell tomorrow. Think how much money we'll make if we sell them all. Come on, Dom."

Twenty-five cents for paper. That left enough money for two long sandwiches at Pierano's. Each sandwich got cut into

153

four pieces. Even if we shared one of them for our own lunch, like we had that day, that left seven to sell, which meant . . . Wow. "A dollar and seventy-five cents!" I shouted.

Gaetano shook his head in amazement. "That's almost double what a grown man makes a day."

"Well, really only a dollar and fifty cents, after we put money in Tin Pan Alley's cup."

"Whoa. He asked for twenty cents, not twenty-five."

"Yeah, but today we only gave him fifteen. And we can afford twenty-five, easy." I spoke fast, before he could object. "How long do you think it'll take us to sell seven sandwiches?"

Gaetano grinned. "We'll have to start earlier."

"But, hey, what if it rains tonight? Where will we put a roll of brown paper?"

Gaetano knitted his brows.

"Where'd you put the pieces of paper we still have left?"

Gaetano pulled them out of his pocket. They were folded up small. "A whole roll is gigantic, though."

"Okay," I said, "here's the plan. We buy three sandwiches at Pierano's tomorrow morning and cut them up. We've already got the paper to wrap them. After we sell those, we can buy the roll of paper and bring it to Grandinetti's. Maybe he'll let us keep it in his store."

"Give me the money." Gaetano held out his hand.

I pulled back. "Why?"

"You can't keep it safe overnight in a barrel."

"I'll put it in a bank, then. You said there were banks everywhere."

"I don't trust these banks," said Gaetano. "No one treats kids fair." He put the fingertips of one hand together and

154

shook them in front of my face. "They'd report us as lost and we'd wind up in an orphanage, and the banks would keep our money. Don't be such a mook. Give it to me."

"No."

"You don't trust me?"

I just looked at him. He'd stolen my documents.

"I asked you a question," said Gaetano.

I took the three quarters from my pocket and handed Gaetano one. "We'll split them overnight."

"Hey, I'm three years older, I should keep two and you keep one."

"The whole thing was my idea," I said.

Gaetano pocketed the quarter and walked off.

Just like that, I was alone again.

And tired. My stomach growled. Lunch had been so small. I had a headache. It was hot. I wanted a midday nap, like back home. People were stupid in America; they didn't know enough to get out of the sun.

Crowds cluttered the sidewalks; it was an effort just to weave my way to the alley. When I got there, the reek hit me like a slap; little piles of trash stewed in the sun-warmed puddles. I put one hand over my nose and mouth and headed for my barrel.

It was gone.

Clank!

I turned around. A big boy with shiny hair had entered the alley and knocked into a stack of debris. Another boy came running up behind him. One look at their faces and I knew they were after me.

I took off in the other direction and fell in rotten vegetables that had turned to slime in the heat.

One boy jumped on my back and rolled me over. He sat on my chest, pinned my arms to my sides with his knees, and pressed both hands over my mouth. The other reached into the pocket with the two quarters, as though he knew what was there. "Is this all of it?" He held a fist in front of my face.

The boy on my chest lifted his hands so I could answer.

"Thief!" I screamed. "Thief, thief!" I thrashed and twisted.

The boy clapped his hands down again and squeezed me with his knees so hard I felt tears come. "Watch who you call names," he said. "Where'd you get all this money? You picked someone's pocket. You're the thief."

"What about the shoes?" said the other boy.

I felt hands fiddling with my shoestrings. No! I kicked and bucked like a wild thing. With every ounce of strength I had, I ripped my arms free and pummeled the boy on top of me. We were rolling in the garbage filth now, all three of us, kicking and punching and biting.

"What's going on there?" came a man's voice.

The thieves ran off.

The man walked toward me. "You okay, kid?"

I got up and swiped at the slime on my pants. Now my hands were slimy, too. "I'm fine."

"You sure? You look pretty bad."

He spoke Napoletano. For an instant I wanted to tell him everything, to beg for help. But then I thought of finding myself in an orphange. "I'm fine." I closed my eyes and pressed the heels of my hands into my eyelids, slime and all. When I opened my eyes, the man was gone.

I had no money.

I had no barrel to sleep in.

Gaetano was right: I was a mook. All that money . . . gone. And it was Tin Pan Alley's and Gaetano's money as much as it was mine.

I hurt—all of me. But my mouth hurt the most. I wiped it. Blood. I ran my tongue around the inside of my mouth. My bottom lip was cut.

And look how stupid I was to still be here. The thieves could come back at any moment. So I went the only place I could go—Grandinetti's store.

He was busy with customers. A broom stood in the corner. I swept, careful to go around people politely, keeping my eyes lowered so no one would take much notice of me. Plums had fallen behind a bushel. I wiped them off and put them neatly back in place. When there was finally a break in the business, Grandinetti leaned against the weighing counter and looked at me. "What happened to you?"

"Nothing."

"Nothing, huh? Nothing that's going to end up as a black eye by morning. And what's that?" He came closer. "A fat lip, too." When I didn't say anything, he walked over to the fruit bushels. "Three tomatoes or an orange. Your choice."

"I need a penny."

He put his hands up in the halt sign. "A few pieces of fruit—that's one thing. But money? I can't afford a paid helper, Dom."

I waved my arm across the room. "Look how nice your floor is now."

"You do good work."

"Just a penny. One penny."

"A penny now. What tomorrow? A nickel? The next day a dime?" He put his hands together as though praying and shook them at me—a gesture I already recognized as his favorite. "I don't make a big profit here. I have to be careful."

"I won't ask for a penny tomorrow."

"I don't know what trouble you're in, Dom. And you seem like a good kid. But . . ."

"I won't ask for a penny tomorrow."

Grandinetti raised both brows. "Promise?"

I hated to promise. What if I still needed a penny tomorrow? But, well, if I did, I'd have to get it someplace else. "I promise."

Grandinetti gave me a penny.

"Thank you."

I walked to the train depot and checked my shoes in baggage overnight. They'd be safer that night than I would be—how funny. I went to Central Park and pawed through trash. All I found were ends of bread smeared with a nasty yellow paste. They barely eased the ache in my gut. And they did nothing for the ache in my head; I'd had two quarters in my pocket and now I had nothing. In the morning I'd have to face Tin Pan Alley and Gaetano. I was pretty sure Tin Pan Alley would forgive me. But Gaetano . . . even if Gaetano didn't punch me, he'd be disappointed. They'd both be disappointed in me. Sick of me. I was sick of me. Me and my big plans. I'd never get home if I kept doing things wrong.

This was too hard. Everything was too hard.

Long before dark, I crawled under the thick bushes by the big pond and slept.

CHAPTER SIXTEEN

More and More Money

"You lost both quarters?" Gaetano shook his head.

"I told you. I was robbed. They jumped me in the alley."

"Both?"

I turned my pockets inside out. "See?"

"What'd they look like, these thieves of yours?"

"One was kind of big. Bigger than you. With slick hair. The other one, I don't know, he was ordinary."

Gaetano smirked. "What are you, blind? No one would pay a cent for information like that." He shook his head. "You look pretty good for someone who got jumped. Your face isn't so hot, but your clothes are clean."

"I woke up before dawn and rinsed my clothes in the pond and washed myself off."

"Your clothes dried that fast?" Gaetano tapped his foot.

I didn't want to tell him that my clothes dried fast because I'd been running around for hours. After I got my shoes out of baggage deposit at the station, I stacked fruit at Grandinetti's and earned a tomato for myself and a badly bruised orange that I shared with Tin Pan Alley at his corner. Gaetano would say it was stupid of me to give Tin Pan Alley oranges. But I was going to give Tin Pan Alley an orange every morning I worked; the look on his face as he ate was worth it. I'd told Tin Pan Alley about the thieves and he didn't get mad—and that was before he knew I had an orange to share. All he said was "I hate thieves." I could tell he'd been robbed before. Lots of times.

I looked at Gaetano now and shrugged. "It's hot out."

Gaetano scratched behind his ear.

"What? You think I hid the money someplace? You don't trust me?"

He grinned. "That's what I asked you yesterday. If you'd given me all the money, we'd be fifty cents richer today. Am I right?"

"Yeah."

He put out his hand. "Trust from now on?"

I shook his hand. "How come you're not crazy mad that our money's gone?"

"*So' cadute l'anielle, ma so' restante 'e ddete*—The rings have fallen away, but our fingers remain—and we've still got the quarter in my pocket. Let's get to work."

That was Uncle Aurelio's kind of optimism—bad things happen, but you don't miss a step. Gaetano could make a decent Jew. I didn't tell him that, though.

We bought the long sandwich at Pierano's and cut it in fourths. The block before we got to Tin Pan Alley's corner, Gaetano stopped. "You stay here with the sandwiches. Let me check things out first."

"Why?"

"His *padrone*. Or don't you remember?"

Oh. I had to confess. "Tin Pan Alley's all right. I saw him this morning. Early. He was alone."

"Oh, yeah?" Gaetano looked hurt. "The two of you are close, huh? Well, I think I'll just go ahead anyway, to check if that *padrone*'s come back."

Right. The *padrone* could have shown up again by this time of morning. I hugged the sandwiches and stood against a building wall. The walkers were so thick I couldn't see past them. I couldn't see Tin Pan Alley's corner.

A woman came out of the nearest door and said something to me in English. I moved over to the next building.

What was keeping Gaetano?

Finally he appeared beside me. "The area's clear."

"And Tin Pan Alley?"

"The mook's playing his triangle. You go sell with him. I'm going to patrol. If I spy his *padrone*, I'll come get you fast."

Over the next hour and a half, we sold four sandwiches, each one for a full quarter, to guys in fancy suits, and no sign of the *padrone*. Soon I sat on the curb outside the paper mill in Chatham Square, waiting while Gaetano bought the roll of brown paper, basking in that day's luck. Two customers had been repeats from the day before. The new ones were friends of theirs. One of them said that if we sold sandwiches at lunch break that day, he'd send down a few

161

of his friends. Tin Pan Alley swore we'd have plenty for everyone.

I could practically feel the ship ticket in my pocket. One thousand sandwiches would be sold in no time. I looked around—yes, good-bye to New York—good riddance.

And out of nowhere there they were: the thieves. I sat tall. The big boy's hair was so slick it glistened in the sun. They stood on the north side of the street, watching. They didn't even have the decency to turn their heads away when our eyes met. I leapt to my feet, but then what? Surely they wouldn't jump me here, in front of everyone. Besides, I had no money on me. The quarters we'd made so far that day were in Gaetano's pocket. My heart beat hard; I wanted to run.

"What's the matter?" Gaetano came out of the factory with the roll of paper in his arms.

I pointed.

Gaetano looked at the boys. They looked back.

"Those are the guys who robbed me."

"Oh yeah? I figured as much. Maurizio's the only thief I know who uses ape snot in his hair." He gave them a wave and walked leisurely toward Park Street.

I walked beside him, looking back at the boys. "Why'd you do that? Why'd you wave as though they're buddies or something?"

"I'm not buddies with anyone," said Gaetano. Then he winked at me. "Except you, that is." He sort of swaggered now. "They stay out of my way, I stay out of theirs."

"They stole some of your money yesterday."

"No, they didn't, not as far as they know. They think they stole your money. They'd never steal mine."

"Why not?"

"My big brother. He'd stab them."

"You have a brother?"

"I told you not to ask about my family."

I could have bitten my tongue.

"Anyway, this time I'll answer, 'cause we're buddies. No. No brother. But they don't know that." He stopped outside Pierano's. "If you ever talk to them, remember: they've done wrong to you, not to me. If they think they got away with robbing me, then nothing protects me anymore. You got it?"

"Can't your big brother protect me, too?"

"Here." He gave me seventy-five cents.

I went into Pierano's, bought three long sandwiches, and came out holding them in a bundle tied together with string.

"Where'd you get the string?" asked Gaetano.

"Pierano tied them. Without my even asking. And he smiled at me. I'm becoming his best customer."

"Not you, you mook. He thinks whoever you're working for is his best customer. You're just a kid."

We walked toward Grandinetti's. I kept looking around for the thieves. "What're we going to do, Gaetano?"

"About what?"

"Our money, for one."

"I can keep the money safe."

"What if you can't?" I said.

"I can. With my big brother's help."

I twisted my fingers through the string around the sandwiches. "Well, what about that roll of paper? You already admitted you don't have anyplace to store it where it won't get rained on."

"I'll come up with something."

I looked over my shoulder again. "The thieves. A block back."

Gaetano didn't say anything.

"They won't know I don't have money on me," I said. "They'll jump me anytime they get me alone."

"After a few times of finding nothing in your pockets, they'll stop."

"I don't want to get jumped. It hurts. Where do they live?"

"What?" said Gaetano in surprise.

"I want to make sure I don't go on their street."

"I can't help you."

"Tell me," I said.

"You don't get it, do you? I don't know where they live, okay? I don't ask. That's how it is with the kids in Five Points." He stuck his finger in my chest. "I'll see you later. For now I've got to come up with a place to stash this roll of paper."

I hadn't realized that *don't ask* was the code of the whole neighborhood. It took a second to sink in. Then I ran and caught up to him. "Grandinetti's," I said. "Remember? That's the perfect place."

"He's Calabrese," said Gaetano. "He might act nice now, but if he gets mad at us, there's no telling what he'll do."

"You're wrong. And he can keep our money safe, too."

"I can keep the money safe," said Gaetano.

"It's going to be a lot soon. Your pockets aren't big enough."

"Stop talking. I've got to think."

We fell into step in silence.

Grandinetti was busy with the morning shoppers. He rushed about, counting out fruits and weighing vegetables and wrapping everything in newsprint from the Italian paper.

But we couldn't wait if we were going to sell sandwiches to the lunch crowd. So I stood behind Grandinetti and whispered, "Can we use the knife?"

"Where? My counter's busy now. You can see that."

"In your storeroom."

He looked at my bundle of long sandwiches. Then he shook his prayer hands at me. "Be careful. Let your friend use the knife." He jerked his chin toward Gaetano. "He's older."

While Gaetano cut the sandwiches, I wrapped them. The pile was high. "How can we carry them all?"

We searched around the storeroom and came up with an empty bushel basket. Gaetano started throwing the sandwiches in it.

My hand stayed his arm. "We have to ask first."

"He likes you. He'll say yes. Especially if the sandwiches are already in it."

"All right. But let me do it." I arranged the sandwiches neatly in three layers.

I went into the main part of the store. There was only one customer left, and she was taking her time choosing lettuce. I tapped Grandinetti on the arm.

He followed me into the storeroom. "What's this?"

"Could we borrow this basket?" I said. "Just for a few hours? Please."

"Okay, but I need it tonight."

"I promise." I gave Grandinetti back his knife. And I handed him a wrapped sandwich—a whole one, not just some small piece. "Lunch," I said with a smile.

Grandinetti looked at me. "You didn't have to do that, Dom."

Gaetano stood the roll of brown paper against the wall of the storeroom. "And we'll leave our paper as security."

"You mean you have no place else to keep it?" Grandinetti turned to me and shook his prayer hands. "Are you trying to be a fox on me? No tricks, you hear?"

"We're just trying to do business," I said. "And we need your help. No tricks."

"All right. You can leave the roll of paper." Grandinetti kept his eyes on me. "Get out of here now."

"Thank you," I said.

Gaetano took one of the wire basket handles and I took the other. We carried the sandwiches out through the store.

Gaetano stopped in the doorway. He looked at me and pointed with his thumb down the street. One of the thieves leaned against a wall, watching Grandinetti's store. "One more thing," said Gaetano to Grandinetti. "Would you walk outside holding that knife and shake it at Dom?"

"What?"

"Then turn toward Chatham Square and shake it high in the air. Like you're threatening someone."

166

"We're putting on a play?" asked Grandinetti.

"Two guys are after me," I said. "One of them's watching."

"Is that how you got the fat lip?"

I nodded.

Grandinetti sighed. "I don't want my customers to see me shaking a knife."

"Then just point it," said Gaetano. "You don't have to shake it."

"All right already. Get out of here." Grandinetti shooed us out the door. He pointed the knife at me. Then he swung it in an arc and pointed toward Chatham Square.

The thief took off running.

Gaetano really was smart.

"And one last thing," said Gaetano.

"*Basta,*" said Grandinetti. "Enough is enough."

"Just a little towel." Gaetano cocked his head and shifted his weight and somehow his whole appearance changed. He seemed much younger, more in need of help. "We have to cover the basket. So no one knows what's in it. Otherwise, kids will snatch sandwiches as we're walking."

Grandinetti slapped his palm on his forehead. Then he put his fists on his hips. "On one condition."

"What?"

"You cut the bull with me. No more phony talk about the paper being security. No more acts. You treat me straight, I'll treat you straight."

Gaetano offered his hand, all grown up again. "Gaetano," he said.

"Francesco," said Grandinetti.

They shook.

Grandinetti took the towel from his shoulder and spread it over the sandwiches. "Get out of here. But have that basket and towel back before I close shop."

Within a few minutes of our arriving at Tin Pan Alley's corner, a trickle of people came out of the buildings. The lunch break was just starting.

"You'd better patrol," I said to Gaetano.

"It's okay," said Tin Pan Alley. "My *padrone* came by while you were gone. I bet he's off eating now." He looked at a passing man. "Sandwiches," he called out in English. "The best in town."

"What's that mean?" I asked. When he told me, I practiced the words under my breath. "Sandwiches. The best in town. Sandwiches. The best in town."

Gaetano unwrapped a whole sandwich and slowly ate it. We hadn't talked about each of us getting a whole sandwich. Now we'd only have eight to sell—but I'd started it by giving Grandinetti a whole sandwich.

I felt faint with hunger. The bigger he chewed, the fainter I felt, but the more sandwiches we sold.

Then it was Tin Pan Alley's turn to eat.

"Sandwiches," I called out. "The best in town."

Gaetano smirked. "Listen to you try to speak English. You sound worse than Tin Pan Alley."

"He sounds good to me," said Tin Pan Alley. "He sounds perfect. Go on, Dom."

"The best in town," I called.

A woman bought a sandwich.

Gaetano stared at me.

I strutted; I couldn't help it.

Then it was my turn to eat. When I'd ordered the sandwiches at Pierano's, I'd thought about getting one without meat. But I figured it wouldn't sell as well. So now I picked out the meat.

Gaetano watched me. "That's not salami. That's ham. What, you don't like ham, either?"

I shook my head.

"Well, don't do the dog routine again."

"Why not?"

"It's not fair. I won't act like a dog, so Tin Pan Alley gets more meat than me. If you're going to give away your ham, give half to me."

"Wait," said Tin Pan Alley. He pulled slices of cheese out of his pocket. "I saved my cheese in case you didn't like the meat today, either. I can trade for your meat."

So I ate my thick cheese sandwich.

We sold out. And still there were people asking for sandwiches.

"We'll have more tomorrow," said Tin Pan Alley in English. "Bring your friends. We'll have lots more." Then he told us what he'd promised.

"Good work. See you tomorrow." I put twenty-five cents in Tin Pan Alley's cup.

He looked at it. "That's five more than we agreed on."

"That's right," said Gaetano. "At least the mook can count."

"Five extra are for yesterday." I didn't look at Gaetano as I spoke. "And tomorrow we'll start earlier and sell more.

So it'll take more of your time. So we'll put more in your cup." I turned and picked up the empty basket.

"You got some weird ways," Gaetano said. "But you're the king. If that's the way you want to play it, okay. Give me the money now."

"It's a dollar and seventy-five cents," I said, tightening my arms around the basket.

"I can count."

"It's way too much to keep in your pocket overnight."

"You're the one who gets robbed, not me."

"Grandinetti could keep it for us," I said.

"We already talked about that," Gaetano growled. "No. Turn it over. Now."

I gave him the money. "Can you spare a penny?"

Gaetano wiped his mouth and looked at me. "If you take a penny, that leaves us a penny short when we go to buy sandwiches tomorrow."

"I mean one of your own pennies. Can you spare one?"

He turned his head away. Then he handed me a penny without even looking at me. "When we split the profits, you owe me." He walked off.

I returned the basket and towel to Grandinetti, checked my shoes into baggage at the train station, and went to Central Park for the night.

CHAPTER SEVENTEEN

Things Go Wrong

We'd made a whole dollar and seventy-five cents. It was like the difference between the sun and the moon—as Uncle Aurelio said. Getting rich in America was easy after all. By my calculations, even after setting aside sandwiches for ourselves (including Grandinetti) on Wednesday, we'd still have two dozen to sell. I went to sleep as happy as anyone curled under a bush in Central Park could be.

But at lunchtime Wednesday it poured in a burst. By the time we managed to take cover under an awning, the top layers of sandwiches in our basket were soaked through so bad, the bread was coming apart. The bottom and side sandwiches were a little soggy. Only four sandwiches from the middle were perfect.

We threw away the bread from the soaked

sandwiches and ate the insides as breakfast. Gaetano wanted to do the same with the soggy ones, too.

"Sell the soggy ones for ten cents each," said Tin Pan Alley. "The secretaries can buy them. At least we come away with something."

"That's mook thinking," said Gaetano. "If we sell a lousy product, we ruin our reputation."

"You think you sound like some kind of hotshot, talking like that," said Tin Pan Alley.

"Hold on." I turned to Tin Pan Alley. "You were the one who said people have to trust food vendors. They trust us so far. If we sell bad stuff, we lose that."

Tin Pan Alley blinked. "Are you on his side now?"

"All I want is to sell sandwiches. Wet sandwiches won't bring us more customers."

"They're not that wet." Tin Pan Alley spat on the ground. He wouldn't look at us. "Okay, then give them to me."

"Pig," said Gaetano. "We'll split them equally."

"You can each take two—one for lunch and one for dinner. But I get the rest."

Tin Pan Alley was the skinniest of us, but still . . . "You're going to get sick," I said.

"I want them."

Gaetano crossed his arms at his chest. "All right. Go puke. But only if we don't have to put money in your cup today."

"Deal," said Tin Pan Alley.

"I'll go patrol," said Gaetano.

"It's okay today. All day long. My *padrone* went to Staten Island. I overheard him tell someone."

172

So we sold the four good sandwiches, then left Tin Pan Alley with six soggy ones.

Gaetano and I walked toward Five Points. We had soggy sandwiches in our pockets, and I had the day's earnings in my fist—a whole dollar. Plus the penny I'd already borrowed from Gaetano for baggage check that night. But about halfway to Grandinetti's I stopped.

"You think he'll make eighty cents by the end of today?"

"That's his problem."

"He's our partner. You even said so. So his problems are our problems."

"How do we really know he's our partner?" said Gaetano. "Maybe he's not going to eat himself sick. Maybe he's selling those sandwiches right now."

"You know he isn't."

Gaetano smirked. "You'll never be a shark, you know that, Dom? You can do the numbers, but you don't have a head for business." He held out his hand with a resigned look on his face.

I gave Gaetano seventy-five cents and the basket to return to Grandinetti. Then I ran back to put twenty-five in Tin Pan Alley's cup.

He wasn't on his corner.

I crossed the street and walked slowly up and down the blocks, listening for his triangle. I never heard him.

When I got to Chatham Square, I saw a boy sitting on a curb ravenously eating a sandwich—one of our soggy ones. He had a small harp wedged under his knees and a tin cup between his feet. He was the boy I'd talked to before, the one with the welts.

I thought of beggar boys all over town eating soggy

sandwiches and feeling like some spirit had blessed them. Munaciello's good counterpart. Nonna would have loved Tin Pan Alley. Before I could think twice, I dropped the twenty-five cents in the boy's cup. He gaped at me. Then he quick tucked the cup between his belly and his knees and went back to eating.

It felt rotten to go to sleep on Wednesday with less money than the night before. We were going backward fast. A thousand sandwiches. How would we ever sell that many? How would I ever make enough money to get home?

I thought of how Mamma used to stand at the window and wave to me when I'd go somewhere with Uncle Aurelio. I felt like she was waving to me that night—waving and calling—only I was too far away to see or hear her. I had to fight to get back to her.

Thursday went okay—so okay, in fact, that at the end of the day we each kept a dime for ourselves. Friday was the same. No thieves or rain. No *padrone*.

The only trouble we had was with the price. Tin Pan Alley would say it clearly. And men who were alone generally paid up, especially if they had suits on. But when there were two men together, or when someone was buying a few sandwiches at once, they gave us a bunch of coins and left fast. The faster they left, the less it turned out they'd paid for each sandwich. And women generally paid less, too, though usually they bargained. That was okay, though. After all, no one but the top guys could really afford twenty-five cents. It was either give a few breaks or lose customers.

Still, by the end of the lunch crowd on Friday, even after putting the money in Tin Pan Alley's cup, we had three dollars and sixty cents.

"Think how many sandwiches we can buy tomorrow," said Gaetano. "It's going to be a good week after all."

"The week is over," I said. "No work on Saturday."

"But Saturday's a workday," Gaetano said. Then he stopped. "I could use a day off."

Tin Pan Alley didn't say anything. I wondered if he ever got a day off.

"A buck a week for a couple of hours' work a day—not bad. Hand over the money," said Gaetano. "I'm about to buy me a steak."

"A buck and twenty cents each," said Tin Pan Alley, putting out his hand, too.

"Hold on." I clamped my hands down on both pockets. "We need something to start next week with."

"A quarter," said Gaetano. "That's what we started this week with."

"Just listen," I said. "If we each take only twenty cents now, we can eat okay Saturday and Sunday, and we'll still have three whole dollars to start Monday with. There's no telling how much money we can make next week if we start with that much." I was already counting the sandwiches we could sell. Why, Monday alone, if luck was on our side, we could eat, and still sell forty-four sandwiches. That couldn't be so. I did the numbers again.

Tin Pan Alley was staring off into the distance. When he turned to me, he nodded and I knew he'd done the numbers, too.

"This is just good business," I said reasonably.

"And you're both out of your minds," said Gaetano. "What's the point of working all the time and never having any fun? Give me my money."

"You'll make a lot more by the end of next week," said Tin Pan Alley almost in a whisper.

"How much more?"

"Tons," I said.

"Aw, come on, guys." Gaetano crossed his arms. "Twenty cents is too little to have any real fun. We have to take at least fifty each." His feet were spread; he was ready for battle.

I thought about it. "Okay, that'll leave us two dollars and ten cents. The extra ten cents won't buy a sandwich. We can put it in Tin Pan Alley's cup."

Tin Pan Alley's eyes shot open wide. "I didn't ask for it."

"You have to work this weekend. We don't."

The first thing I did with my money was pay back Gaetano the three cents I'd borrowed to check my shoes. Then I set aside seven more cents to pay for my shoes for the next week.

I spent the weekend in Central Park, eating popcorn and meat on sticks. Forty cents went a long way.

Monday we discovered the problem with buying two dollars' worth of sandwiches: once we cut them and wrapped them up nice, the basket couldn't hold them all. So Gaetano carried the basket with most of them, and I carried an armful.

When we got to the bottom of Mulberry Street, I dropped one. Gaetano was already crossing the street, and he didn't see. I could pick it up fast and wipe off the paper and no one would know the difference.

I shifted the others to one arm, reached down with my free hand, and dropped two more. A dog appeared out of nowhere and ran off with one. Then something knocked me from behind, and my chin smacked hard on the side-walk. I rolled over in time to see the two thieves make off with the rest of my sandwiches.

By the time I caught up to Gaetano, he was halfway down the next block.

"What happened? Where are the sandwiches?"

"A dog got one. And the two thieves got the others. I guess your big brother isn't protecting you anymore."

"Sure he is. He's just not protecting you. You have to stay by my side or they can get you." He cocked his head at me. "Cheer up. We've still got a basketful to sell. Find some paper in that pile of trash and wipe off your chin. No one's going to buy from a bleeding kid."

While Gaetano patrolled the area, Tin Pan Alley and I sold twenty-three sandwiches, clearing four dollars and sixty cents after putting twenty-five in Tin Pan Alley's cup. A great day.

Gaetano put out his hand. "A dollar. Right now."

"We agreed to go another week."

"We doubled our money in one day. I want my dollar."

I threw up my hands and let them slap to my sides. "If everything went just right—if everyone paid us twenty-five cents and if we sold every sandwich—our money wouldn't just double in a day, it would grow by . . ." I thought. "Four times!" The numbers were staring me in the face. "We've got to keep the money in there till the end of the week." That was the fastest way to get to a thousand sandwiches.

"Oh, all right." Gaetano crossed his arms. "Give me twenty cents."

On Tuesday we bought sixteen long sandwiches. Pier-ano's eyes practically popped out of his head. He gave me a breakfast pastry, and one for Gaetano, too, who was out on the sidewalk looking in through the window. When I dared to mention we worked with a third guy, Pierano dropped another pastry in the bag.

Once we cut the sandwiches, we were way past what the bushel basket could hold. We begged Grandinetti to lend us his one-wheeled handcart. He wasn't happy about it, but so long as we got it back to him by three o'clock, with the towel, it was okay. And he smiled when we gave him a sandwich.

Gaetano pushed the cart and I walked beside him. The mound of sandwiches under the towel was impressive— more than sixty. I watched it proudly. Mamma, here I come.

At the bottom of Mulberry Street, I was on the lookout for that dog and the two thieves. They weren't around. But four little boys—the oldest couldn't have been more than six—came up begging. They had on nothing but short pants. I tried to shoo them away. Gaetano bumped the cart down the curb and crossed the street as though they weren't there.

As he was maneuvering the cart up the other curb, one of the urchins pulled off the towel and they all grabbed sandwiches with both hands and ran back through the traffic across the street. I raced after them, but they split up. I ran back to Gaetano.

"You didn't catch any of them?" he practically shouted.

"I didn't want to leave you alone, with no one to help you guard the cart."

"Yeah, like you're some big help." Gaetano pushed the cart fast, his bottom lip thrust forward.

"We've still got gobs to sell," I said.

But he fumed all the way to Wall Street.

Tin Pan Alley ate the pastry from Pierano's while Gaetano went on and on about what a mess I'd made of things, his temples pulsing.

"Why are you so mad?" I finally said. "You didn't act like this when the thieves jumped me yesterday."

"This is a lot worse, you mook. When those *scugnizzi* tell all the other *scugnizzi* we're easy targets, we'll be mobbed every morning."

"So let's just tell the *scugnizzi* about your big brother."

"You think they don't know? Those kids listen to everything. But, you see, big brothers don't beat up *scugnizzi*. They're too little."

"My *padrone* doesn't care how old someone is," said Tin Pan Alley. "He beats anyone."

"Exactly," said Gaetano. "A *padrone* is the lowest of the low. My big brother is honorable."

His big brother. Who didn't even exist.

Gaetano stomped off, scowling, to patrol the area, while Tin Pan Alley and I waited for the lunch crowd to come trickling out of the buildings.

But today they rushed, and they didn't give us a second glance. A woman who'd been our customer twice before scurried past with a cloth sack full of small banners on sticks.

"What's going on?" I asked Tin Pan Alley.

He ran after the woman and they talked.

When Gaetano realized something was wrong, he joined me at the cart.

Tin Pan Alley came back, his face striken. "It's Flag Day."

"Never heard of it," said Gaetano.

"It's celebrating the country."

"You mook, Independence Day's not till July."

"You're the mook. It's Flag Day. Some new thing. The woman said so. Everyone's going to the public schools to see their kids march in a parade holding little flags."

"Do you know where the schools are?" I asked Gaetano. Gaetano smirked. "Around here? What do you think?"

"It doesn't matter, anyway," said Tin Pan Alley. "Lunch is part of the celebration."

We watched as more customers went on by.

Gaetano kicked the sidewalk. "So what are we supposed to do with all this food?"

"Not everyone has kids." I took the handles and pushed the cart a few steps. "Let's go door-to-door to the little businesses. I pass tons of them on the way to Central Park every night."

"No one's going to pay what Wall Street pays," said Tin Pan Alley. "The rest of the world is poor."

"So let them pay less," said Gaetano. "Otherwise, the whole day is a flop. And since you"—he pointed at me—"and you"—he pointed at Tin Pan Alley—"wouldn't let us keep back any of yesterday's profits, that means good-bye, business." He grabbed the cart handles from me and rolled back toward Five Points. "Come on," he called over his shoulder.

"I can't leave," said Tin Pan Alley. "My *padrone*."

Gaetano stopped and turned around with a bulldog face. "We need you to speak English. Get over here."

Tin Pan Alley didn't move.

"Sandwiches," I said in English. "The best in town."

"Please," Tin Pan Alley said to me in English.

"What's that mean?"

"It's a good word. When you walk into a store, begin with *please*. And end with *thank you*."

I knew what *thank you* meant. "Please," I said. "Thank you." I gave Tin Pan Alley two sandwiches—one for lunch, one for dinner—but I didn't have any coins to put in his cup.

Gaetano and I rolled up the street. We stopped in every little store we passed, all the way to Chatham Square. Then we went around the edge of Five Points, to avoid the *scugnizzi*, and back along Canal Street. Then north along the route I took to the train station. It was well past lunchtime when we stopped to eat. We'd sold all but ten sandwiches. Most for ten cents. But sometimes we were lucky and got fifteen.

I chewed on a cheese sandwich and looked over at the last ones on the cart. My heart fell. "What'll we do with the rest?"

"If I have to eat another of these sandwiches for dinner," said Gaetano, "I'll puke." He jammed the rest of his in his mouth. "I dreamed of sandwiches last night."

I believed him; I had, too. "We could give them away."

"No one would take them. They'd figure there was something wrong with them."

We looked at each other and burst out laughing.

So we kept hawking, even though it was the middle of the afternoon. We sold two more. Then I told Gaetano about what Tin Pan Alley had done with the soggy sandwiches the Wednesday before, and we walked around putting sandwiches in the cups of beggar boys.

Once we finally counted our money, we had five dollars and fifteen cents.

Gaetano moved close to me and hunched over so no one could see what was in his hands. He counted the money again. Then he stuck it in his pocket. "I can't believe it. I couldn't believe it yesterday when it grew so fast. But today—with everything that went wrong—it should have gone down to nothing."

"We started the morning with a ton of sandwiches, Gaetano. We couldn't wind up empty-handed."

"But this isn't how money works." Gaetano shook his head. "I know what you said yesterday. All that stuff about quadrupling. But that isn't how money works, really. If you make a dollar one day, you make another dollar the next, not five." He patted the outside of his pocket. "You really think this will keep up?" he whispered.

"If we buy more sandwiches each day, we'll make more money than the day before. Lots more."

"We can't sell more sandwiches. There aren't enough customers at Tin Pan Alley's corner on a regular day."

"You're right. Pretty soon we can save some of our money."

"Or spend it."

Right. We'd sell one thousand sandwiches in no time. The money was coming in. And I'd spend mine on documents and a ticket before long.

CHAPTER EIGHTEEN

Signora Esposito

We crossed the street in stunned silence. Even though I understood the numbers . . . Five dollars and fifteen cents. Wow. "We need a bank," I said finally. "We need Grandinetti."

We went up Mulberry to Grandinetti's without another word. There were a couple of women in the store, and Grandinetti looked at us through the window and shook his head. So we waited out on the sidewalk.

When the customers finally left, I rolled the handcart into the storeroom. I picked loose produce off the floor and arranged it into piles. I jerked my chin toward the corner where the broom stood. Gaetano took the broom and swept. Neither of us said anything.

Grandinetti scratched the back of his neck and

watched us. Then he took out a pencil and walked around the store, making a check of inventory. Finally, he brushed his hands off and put them on his hips. "Okay, I get it. You're trying to make up, but it won't work."

Make up? And suddenly I realized. "I'm sorry we were late."

"And where's my towel?"

"Some kids stole it."

"That's it," said Grandinetti. "I can't lend you my things anymore. They're too important to me."

"How much does the handcart cost?" asked Gaetano.

"I traded for it—used. But to replace it, I'd have to pay two dollars and fifty cents."

"Let us keep it," said Gaetano. He put two dollars and fifty cents on the counter. "Buy a new cart. It's a good deal for you."

I gulped.

Gaetano reached in his pocket again. "And, hey, here's ten more cents for the towel."

Grandinetti blinked. "How'd you get so much money?"

"The sandwich business is good," said Gaetano.

"That good?"

Gaetano emptied his pockets onto the counter.

"Will you keep our money for us at night?" I said.

Grandinetti slowly counted it. "Give it to your mother."

"He can't," said Gaetano. "She's not here."

"You told me you don't have a father." Grandinetti wiped his nose with the back of his hand. "Now is Gaetano saying you don't have a mother, either?"

"Sure I have a mother," I said. "In Napoli."

Grandinetti threw up his hands. "I'm not getting mixed

up with a *padrone*. If you don't want to give the money to your *padrone*, you'll have to find some other solution."

"I don't have a *padrone*."

Grandinetti stared at me. "You're alone?"

"I've got Gaetano," I said. "And Tin Pan Alley."

"Who?"

"Another kid," said Gaetano.

"Where's your father?" Grandinetti asked Gaetano.

"Dead."

I winced.

"And your mother?"

"She died when I was born."

I clenched my teeth to keep from making a noise. Poor Gaetano. Had he come to America with his father, and then had his father died on him? But I could never ask him. I stared at the floor.

"Let me get this straight. You boys are on your own? Neither one of you has family or a *padrone* here?"

We didn't say anything.

"Where do you sleep?"

"I used to have a barrel," I said. "But now I sleep in the park."

Grandinetti looked at Gaetano. "And you?"

"I take care of myself."

Grandinetti shook his head in disgust. "There's too much of this going on. Too many kids on their own." He put the money back in Gaetano's hand. "Here's what you do. Cross the street and go to number forty-four, one flight up. Rent a room from Signora Esposito."

"How much does a room cost?" I asked.

"It's not a real boardinghouse. She has one extra room.

185

Tiny. Offer her two dollars a week per person, with dinner included."

"We can't afford that," said Gaetano.

"Did you really earn this money?"

"Yes."

"Are you planning on earning more?"

"Yes."

"Then what are you talking about? It's half the price of even the cheapest boardinghouses." Grandinetti handed us each a plum. "Now get out of here. I'm going to stand in this doorway and watch. Go to the widow's. I mean it. If you sleep outdoors with money in your pockets, you'll wake with empty pockets—if you have any clothes on at all, that is."

We walked up Mulberry, reading the numbers.

Gaetano checked over his shoulder. "Grandinetti's still watching us."

"It doesn't matter whether he watches or not," I said. "He's right. We're going to keep earning money. We need a safe place at night. A home."

"Wherever I am is my home."

"That's what you say. I saw the policeman chasing you."

Gaetano looked stung. "What I have is a lot better than the park."

"I hope so." Here it was: number forty-four. I opened the door.

Gaetano stopped on the sidewalk.

Signora Esposito had an apartment one flight up. Was she young? As young as Mamma? Her hair was bound to be black. But was it wavy or curly? Did her hands rest easy or was she always crocheting or chopping vegetables? Was she fat? Thin? Tall? Short? Were there other people there? Children? Did they have things to play with?

It felt like forever since I'd been in a real home. I had to see this one. And she had to take us in. "Come on."

"I'll look. One quick look. That's all." Gaetano followed me up the stairs.

I knocked on the first door. No one answered.

"There's another door," said Gaetano.

So we went to the second door and knocked.

"Who's there?" came a high voice. It wavered, like a singer's. I imagined her willowy and graceful.

"Dom and Gaetano," I said. "Grandinetti—the fruit vendor—he sent us."

The sound of a chain being unlatched came from the other side of the door. I held my breath.

And there she was: the widow I'd seen in Grandinetti's last Monday morning—the one who had watched him like a hawk, as though he was going to cheat her. She had on a robe and her face wasn't powdered, but she still looked scary, like a ghost. "What do you want?" said the hag.

I couldn't speak. Gaetano gave me a little punch in the kidneys. "*Aiii*," burst from me. "Grandinetti said you might have a room for rent."

She examined Gaetano from head to toe. Then me. When she got to my shoes, she nodded. "My children are grown. There's three beds in the room." She stepped back. "Well, are you going to come in or not?" She patted her hair nervously. It was black with gray streaks and it looked hard and dry as straw.

The door opened into her kitchen. A pot of bones simmered on the stove. I wondered if she'd collected them

187

from garbage cans. We followed her across a dark, cluttered living room and down to the end of a narrow hall. She opened a door.

It was a sunny room with a set of drawers, three beds, a tattered rug. The mirror was chipped. The sheets were patched. The wallpaper hung free in one corner. There was no extra space anywhere. Everything in the room felt old and well used and homey. You could sleep in that room without wondering what might crawl over you in the night.

"We'll take it," said Gaetano. "A dollar fifty a week, with dinner."

I glared at Gaetano. He'd seen the pot of bones, too. He knew she was poor.

She pulled on a limp lock of hair. "A dollar fifty won't pay for dinner every night."

"Two dollars," I said. "Each."

She pursed her lips and now her eyes grew shrewd. "That's still not much."

"And we'll do odd jobs." I pointed at the wallpaper. "You could use extra hands around here."

She put out her palm. "Four dollars total, then. Due every Tuesday."

Gaetano stepped in front of me. "Is dinner ready?"

"What do you think I am, a fortune-teller? I had no idea you'd be coming tonight. There's barely enough for me."

"Then we'll pay tomorrow night," said Gaetano. "At dinner. And we'll pay less this time because we're getting one meal less. We'll pay three dollars."

Signora Esposito sucked in her breath. I could see in her eyes she was trying to figure out if she was getting cheated.

"Three fifty," I said.

"Very well."

So that night I stretched out in a bed. Back in Napoli I'd slept on two chairs pushed together. Since then I'd slept in all kinds of places: the floor under Eduardo's bunk on the cargo ship, the top deck of the *Città di Napoli*, the barrel, Central Park.

A bed. My own bed. I put my shirt and pants neatly in a drawer, careful to keep my underthings on—Mamma had said, "Don't undress with anyone around"—and slid beween the clean sheets.

We had plenty of money to start out our business day in the morning. Lunch the next day would be a sandwich. And dinner would be whatever Signora Esposito made, which was bound to be something different from a Pierano sandwich.

"Everything's going our way," I whispered into the night air.

Gaetano didn't answer. I could tell from his breathing that he wasn't asleep. But if he wanted to pretend, that was okay with me. Maybe I'd spooked him. After all, you could invite bad fortune merely by thinking life was good.

I rolled on my side. The mattress yielded, like the stuffing in the chairs back in Napoli. The bed frame creaked. Had the chairs creaked when I rolled back home? I couldn't remember. How could that be?

Panic made my throat narrow. I had trouble breathing. I sat up in the dark to try to get more air. I should still remember everything about Napoli. Every detail. How long had I been gone? Was it two months? I could remember if I tried hard enough.

Okay, I'd start with Nonna's proverbs. I imagined her sitting at the kitchen table, crocheting, her tiny hands moving so fast, saying, *"O cane mozzeca 'o stracciato"*—The dog bites whoever dresses in rags. I lay on my stomach and reached under my pillow to rest my hands on my shoes. These shoes kept me from looking like I was dressed in rags. Signora Esposito had given us the room because of them. One more way these shoes had paved my path.

A recipe now, I could remember a recipe for sure. Spaghetti puttanesca. Aunt Sara made it best. She put tomatoes in a bowl and poured boiling water over them. In another bowl she put our secret ingredient—a couple of handfuls of raisins, with boiling water over them, too. She pitted black olives and sliced them. And chopped a few cloves of garlic. Then put olive oil in the pan and crushed in a couple of dried red peppers. When the pepper smoke made us cough, she added anchovy fillets, smushing them with the back of a spoon till they came apart in the oil. Then the olives and garlic and a spoonful of capers. She peeled the tomatoes—the skin came off easy after they'd been sitting in the hot water—and cut them into the pan with a pinch of salt. She drained the raisins and threw them in. And it was done. Ready to pour over spaghetti with chopped parsley on top.

I was remembering everything. Breath came easy now. I could remember.

I could see Uncle Vittorio, tall and thin and sallow. I could feel the thick calluses on the scoop of palm between his thumb and first finger on both hands, from holding that broom he swept the streets with every night. I could smell horse in Uncle Aurelio's hair and see the burn scars from the smithy fire on his knuckles. I could see Aunt Rebecca tucking my cousins into bed, and Luigi and Ernesto protesting—"Just one more story!" She'd sit on the edge of the bed, her jutting jaw moving slowly as she told about a silly man who saw the reflection of the moon in a pond and thought the moon itself was in the water. The whole of her wide girth would jiggle when she laughed.

And, at last, I saw Mamma. The inside of my nose prickled with held-back tears. Mamma in front of a window, light flooding around her. She was beautiful and warm and soft and strong and anise-sweet. And she was crying.

I had to work hard and earn my ticket fast. One thousand sandwiches. That wasn't so far away now—not at this rate. And I had to spend the last hour of every day going over everything I could remember from Napoli so that I'd recognize it all when I finally got home. That way it would be just as though I'd never been gone at all.

She'd be proud of me when I got home, proud to know I'd been my own boss.

I pressed the heels of my hands on my eyelids.

"You okay?" Gaetano sat up now.

I didn't answer.

"What you told Grandinetti, about having a mother back in Napoli, well . . . I figured she was dead. You know, died on the ship over. A lot of women do." He went silent.

"She's not dead. She paid my passage on a cargo ship."

"Cargo ships don't take passengers. Oh! You mean you were a stowaway. She put you as a stowaway, all alone! What kind of mother would do a thing like that?"

"What are you saying? That's not how it was. She was supposed to come with me, but this bad guy on the cargo ship wouldn't let her."

"What'd he do to her?"

"I don't know. He told me to go hide and he said he'd hide her someplace else. And then she was gone."

"Sounds like she wanted you to go alone."

"Don't say that!"

"You said it yourself."

"I did not. You stinker!"

"You said she paid your passage. She didn't pay her own passage."

"That's not true! Shut up!" My heart was beating so hard, I couldn't hear anything else. I dropped back on my pillow and listened to the drum in my head.

After a long time, Gaetano said, "Yeah, what do I know?" He lay down on his side. "Good night, Dom."

My head was finally quiet.

Why did I tell Gaetano that Mamma had paid for my passage instead of saying our passage? Was that really what I'd heard her tell Franco when she was arguing with him? I couldn't remember.

I went over that last morning in Italy. Mamma dressed me in my Sabbath clothes, with my new socks and shoes. Like a traveler. She wore an ordinary dress. And she carried nothing extra. No bundle of treasures, none of the things that the immigrants at Ellis Island carried.

But I was her treasure. I was all she needed.

She didn't mean for me to go alone. No one would think a nine-year-old could make it on his own. Sure, Rosaria, Tonino's oldest daughter, was taking care of her four younger brothers while he made his fortune in America—and she was my age. But Rosaria had neighbors and relatives who looked in on her. I was alone. Mamma would never have stowed me away alone.

The smell of a citronella candle came through the open window. And I remembered Mamma crying. She had cried for three nights in a row. I was going to ask her why, but each morning when we woke, I'd forget.

The heels of my hands pressed so hard on my eyeballs, I saw white inside my head.

"Chi tene mamma, nun chiagne"—Whoever has a mother doesn't cry. One of Nonna's proverbs.

I had a mother. And she hadn't put me on the boat alone on purpose. She wouldn't have. She couldn't have.

She loved me. Mamma loved me.

I got out of bed and shut the window.

CHAPTER NINETEEN

A Way of Life

I woke up early and staggered in the dark through the apartment door to the bathroom out in the hall. I felt like a king on a throne—ha! The king of Mulberry Street, doing my business in the right kind of place again. No more hiding behind bushes.

The door opened while I was finishing up.

"What? Who's there? What do you think you're doing here?" A man swiped me on the shoulder, knocking me to the floor. My cheek hit something sharp. "Get out of here, you ruffian!" He kicked me in the side. He grabbed me by the elbow and threw me out in the hall.

"Help!" I screamed.

"Out, out, out!" He pulled me up by the hair and dragged me to the top of the steps.

"Stop!" Signora Esposito came running and blocked the stairwell. "Let go of him!"

"He was in the bathroom. A hoodlum in our bathroom!"

"That's no hoodlum. That's Dom. Let go!"

"Dom?"

"He's renting a room from me. Dom. And his friend, Gaetano."

The man let go of my hair. "My mistake." He brushed off his hands as though I'd gotten him dirty. "Next time, let a person know when there's someone new around."

"Next time ask before you beat someone senseless." Signora Esposito took me by the hand and pulled me inside.

She roughly washed the cut on my cheek and tsked. "Look at that."

"It doesn't hurt," I lied. It had been a long time since anyone had fussed over me, even gruffly. If she kept it up, I might cry.

She took out a bottle of red-brown tincture and smeared it on me.

I tensed up. But it didn't even sting.

"When's the last time you cleaned yourself?"

I shrugged.

"Tonight after dinner take a sponge bath in the kitchen sink."

"Thank you. I might do that."

"You will do that," she said.

When Gaetano finally woke, he took one look at my face and let out a low whistle.

So I told him the whole story, maybe exaggerating a bit

for sympathy. I held the darkening bruise on my elbow under his nose.

"You look terrible." Gaetano looked like he was fighting a smile. "He beat you up in the bathroom. That's awful, but . . ." He laughed. Then he jumped out of bed and clapped his hands. "This is great. This is exactly what we needed."

"What are you talking about?"

"You'll see."

We went to Pierano's and bought ten long sandwiches. He didn't throw in free pastries that day, but he did ask me about my cut. I shrugged. Later, when Grandinetti asked, I told him. Some things only friends could understand.

The mound of sandwiches on the cart was smaller than it had been the day before. But who cared? This was our cart—ours.

It was on Park Street that I realized the two thieves were following us on the other side of the street.

"Hey . . . ," I said to Gaetano.

"I know." At the corner he crossed—but toward the thieves. He beckoned them over.

They walked up, Maurizio taking the lead. "Where you taking those sandwiches every day?"

"Not that far," said Gaetano. "You know any little kids that need a job?"

Maurizio smoothed back his hair. "Who's hiring?"

"The boss." Gaetano jerked his chin toward my cheek and held out my arm so the bruise showed. "And spread the word: he doesn't put up with monkey business."

Maurizio smiled meanly. "You have a *padrone*! I never thought you'd go that way, of all people."

"Hell no," Gaetano yelped. "Boss—not *padrone*." He moved closer to Maurizio. *"Chi tene 'a libertà è ricco e nun 'o sape"*—Whoever is free is rich, though he doesn't know it.

"Who is it? Who's your boss?"

Gaetano just looked at him.

"Someone from outside Five Points?"

"We got to go. Oh, here. From the boss." Gaetano gave Maurizio two sandwiches. "And something for your little friends." He gave him four more.

Maurizio stood there with his arms full, gaping.

"That's the last time. Understand? I'm counting on you to keep those kids in line." We walked off.

"You didn't even introduce me," I said.

"It wasn't a social call. Anyway, they know your name. You won't get jumped again. And no *scugnizzi* will come near this cart."

Between the sandwiches Gaetano gave away and the ones we ate, Tin Pan Alley and I had only thirty to sell. But they all went, most for full price. At the end of the day, Gaetano and I went back to Signora Esposito's with six dollars and ten cents.

We set aside two dollars and fifty cents for starting the next day. After paying our room and board, we had only ten cents left. And we owed Tin Pan Alley his share of the day's profits.

But Thursday and Friday went fine. Just the usual annoyances—people who paid less than full price; a man who dropped his sandwich, then demanded another for free.

In the next month, business grew so fast, it was like an eruption of Mount Vesuvio. It felt as though Wall

Street had been doing nothing but waiting for our sandwiches.

Part of what made it work was that Gaetano was a champion patroller. He spotted Tin Pan Alley's *padrone* every time, and whisked me and the cart away fast.

And part of what made it work was that Tin Pan Alley listened, and he told us everything, and we learned. One day one of the men who had bought a sandwich going into work that morning came back and asked for a second at a reduced price. He offered fifteen cents. We settled on eighteen. He said he'd eaten the first one as his breakfast.

That afternoon I dragged Gaetano with me to Mott Street to talk the Cassone grandma into making a potato and fried egg sandwich on a long loaf—with rosemary and pepper—specially for us the next morning. We paid her twenty-five cents. When we picked it up, the bread was jammed full. We figured most people couldn't eat even a quarter of such heavy stuff that early in the morning, so we cut it into six pieces to sell for twenty cents each. It was a gamble—but all we had to do was sell two of the six pieces to come out on top. We wound up selling them for twelve cents—but we sold out.

We ordered two breakfast sandwiches from Old Lady Cassone for the next day. And more after that. And the next week, we added breakfast pastries to the cart. That was Gaetano's idea. For some crazy reason, people would say egg sandwiches were too rich, then they'd turn right around and buy cannoli stuffed with ricotta. They bought all of it. Pierano now sold us sandwiches cheaper—twenty-three cents each—because we bought so many.

After the breakfast shift, Gaetano and I ran back to Park

Street to get ready for the lunch crowd, which was much bigger.

One noon, in midsummer, a man in a regular top hat and sporting a small, neat beard asked me if any of our sandwiches came without cheese. By this time I spoke half-decent English when it came to sandwiches. Gaetano was at my side. He understood well enough by then, too, and he muttered to me in Napoletano that the guy ought to learn how to pick out the cheese. The man wasn't Italian, and I doubt he understood a word of what Gaetano said, but he understood the tone. He went away without waiting for my answer. There was something about him. It wasn't just his way of walking or dressing or his beard or that look of being offended on his face—it was all of those things together. I made a guess about him.

The next day I watched for the man. When I saw him come out of a building, I ran over. "What kind meat you want?" I asked in English.

"Beef," he said. "Just beef."

"Polish?" I asked.

He looked alarmed. "Why do you say that? I'm not Polish."

"Polish beef—it is best," I said.

He hesitated. Then he said, "That's true."

"Come tomorrow," I said. "But you got buy three sandwiches. That how we make—three at a time." It wasn't true. But I figured I'd eat the fourth one.

"I can buy three," he said. "Friends will eat them."

When I went back to the cart, Tin Pan Alley whispered to me, "There's a Polish butcher on Baxter Street."

Surprised, I moved close to him so Gaetano couldn't

hear us. "How'd you do that? How'd you guess what he wanted?"

"Same way you did, probably."

So I learned that Gaetano had been wrong about Five Points; it wasn't only Italians. Just as Chinese were moving in to Mott Street, Poles were moving in, too—Jews. And Grandinetti had told me Five Points had been Irish before it was Italian.

We sold a fair number of kosher sandwiches after that. Only, Tin Pan Alley didn't call them kosher. He called them pure beef, and our eyes locked in understanding when he'd hawk them that way.

Every time I went to Baxter Street to pick up the beef, I passed doorways with *mezuzahs*. Even the butcher shop had a *mezuzah*. My fingers itched to touch them, but I never did. Then I'd run back to Grandinetti's, stopping at the bakery for loaves, and I'd pile the sandwiches high with beef and rings of red onion. Gaetano didn't give me any trouble about it, even though he found out pretty fast where I bought the beef. Business was business.

In the late afternoon we sold produce from Grandinetti's. The Wall Street workers would buy a single carrot, two tomatoes, a handful of lettuce leaves. Our customers were happy with the vegetables. When I told Grandinetti, he said Germans and Irish and Swedes and all of them might know how to make money, but they had never known how to eat. Italians, now, Italians, they knew how to eat. He said, "That's how we'll change America." Gaetano laughed, but Grandinetti was serious. It was his big dream—to teach America how to eat.

It was summer, and everything grew. But we could look

ahead and see that we'd better figure out new things to sell if we wanted to have customers in autumn. So we added candied almonds and other sweets.

We learned, sometimes the hard way. Once we got rained out. We had bought an oilcloth and we kept it in the cart so we could cover everything at the first drop. But this rain lasted all through the lunch hour and all afternoon, and almost no one came out to buy. After that we scanned the sky before going into Pierano's.

Another time a wheel broke off the front of our cart on the way to Wall Street and half the load fell in the gutter, ruined. So we began checking the cart.

We brought leftovers home to Signora Esposito. At first the widow cooked bad. Her habits were stingy. Her white face wasn't powdered—it was floured. Flour cost less than powder. And her strong perfume covered the fact that she hardly ever washed, to save on water and soap. But once she learned to count on our rent, she bought better food and turned out to be a pretty good cook. She smiled sometimes. And she even started to use an iron to curl her hair when she went to church.

The best thing about her was that I asked her never to make pork or horsemeat or shellfish, and she didn't say a word about it to Gaetano. I was so grateful, I bought her rhinestone clips for her hair. The funny thing was, on that same day Gaetano bought her a box of real talcum. I don't know what secret she was keeping for him.

By late summer the cart was too full to keep racing off whenever Gaetano spotted the *padrone*. And it upset our customers. So we set up across the street, catty-corner to Tin Pan Alley. He hawked for us on his side, and I hawked

201

on the other. Gaetano still patrolled most of the time, but whenever he saw the *padrone,* all he had to do was signal Tin Pan Alley to play his triangle.

Having all those customers made another change for us—a funny one, because what Gaetano had made up that day, telling Maurizio that our "boss" needed more kids, turned out to be true. Sometimes the orders came in such a rush that Gaetano had to quit patrolling and Tin Pan Alley had to cross the street and still the three of us couldn't fill them fast enough. We hired kids from Five Points to help. Usually Michele, Nicola, and Roberto. They were brothers about a year apart. They worked fast. But more important, they were honest. It was my job to count up the sums for each transaction—out loud, so customers knew they were getting a fair deal.

All three of us came up with ideas. But somehow I was in charge. Maybe because Gaetano and Tin Pan Alley really didn't like each other. In any case, I was the boss. We never let on about that, of course. Whenever we'd hire a new kid for the day, I'd say something to Gaetano like, "You think the boss would take this one on?"

And Gaetano would answer, "If he can clean up his face and hands good, I bet the boss'll say okay."

No one messed with us; this boss had gotten a grip on Gaetano, the most independent guy in the neighborhood, so he had to be a real terror.

One day we hired an older boy to help out. He demanded twenty-five cents for working the lunch shift, when the little boys were happy with only ten. But he spoke English and he looked clean, so we did it. The very next day he appeared on the same block as us with four sandwiches in his arms. He sold them for twenty cents each. The day after that, he came with twelve sandwiches.

We lowered our price to fifteen cents a sandwich. Then ten. Then five. It meant we lost money, so much that we had to pay Signora Esposito in installments. She didn't ask why; she knew the code, too—don't ask. But we could afford to lose money for a while, and the other boy couldn't. He disappeared, and our prices went back up.

Gaetano still wouldn't speak English no matter what. Once we stepped out of Five Points, I did the talking.

Tin Pan Alley still played his triangle and whistled when we were off restocking the cart. He didn't have to, though. By this point we put as much as he needed in his cup at the end of the day to make eighty cents. He was a great hawker. He wore a smile all the time and was friendly with the customers.

We never worked on Saturday, the Sabbath. The rest of New York, it seemed, worked six days a week, but not us.

Gaetano didn't complain. He missed his old job of being information man for the neighborhood, so on weekends he eavesdropped and scouted to his heart's content. Weekends were fun time—that was what he said.

Tin Pan Alley didn't complain, either, because he never complained.

I spent Saturday at the wharves, looking at ships. I'd be on one soon enough.

And Sundays, well, I never set foot in a church again, even though Gaetano and Signora Esposito scolded me. I lay on my bed with my pillow over my head and let them blabber. When they finally left for church, I'd go out for an adventure.

Sometimes I stopped in at Catholic mutual aid societies to snatch a few pastries. And during saint festivals I walked happily through the crowds. People sold all sorts of crazy things. But Riccardo, a guy who made girls swoon, sold the very craziest thing. He wore a dark suit, but from his pockets colored ribbons sprouted in profusion. He'd lean toward a woman, who would put her nose to his neck, then drop a coin in his hand. At every *festa* Riccardo sold sniffs of himself.

But mostly I spent my Sundays walking around the island of Manhattan alone. The air was fresh and my stomach was full. Had Mamma gotten an office job yet? If she had, everyone in my family had a full stomach. That was good. That way they wouldn't be so sad all the time from missing me.

CHAPTER TWENTY

Pietro

One lunch shift a big ham of a hand clutched the neck of Tin Pan Alley's shirt.

"Hey," I shouted, looking up.

His *padrone*! He dragged him off. Tin Pan Alley didn't make a squeak.

"Shut up," Gaetano whispered in my ear. "If you make a scene, Tin Pan Alley will pay worse for it. And anyway, you'll embarrass him."

I watched while they disappeared around a corner. Tin Pan Alley didn't look back. My stomach turned. "You think it'll be bad?"

Gaetano just looked at me.

The next morning Tin Pan Alley told us his *padrone* had beaten him for doing something without permission and demanded he bring in two dollars a day from then on. He said Tin Pan Alley could make that much easy working at our cart. He never guessed Tin Pan Alley was getting a third of our profits—all saved in a wooden box back in the bedroom at Signora Esposito's. Tin Pan Alley laughed at that. But when a customer yanked on his shirtsleeve later to get his attention, I saw him wince.

So when the breakfast shift was over, I said, "Pull up your shirt." His open wounds made me gasp. Even Gaetano, who had never said a friendly word to Tin Pan Alley, was so furious, I thought the pulsing in his temples would burst.

That night after supper I sat on my bed in our room and said, "We have to help him escape."

"You're such a mook." Gaetano paced around the small floor. "It might even be illegal." He opened the window higher. "Maybe it would be a kind of kidnapping." He punched his right fist into his left palm. "No one has ever crossed a *padrone* and gotten away with it." He paced some more. Then he stopped and looked away. I wondered how much he really disliked Tin Pan Alley, and how much that dislike was behind his words now. When he finally looked back at me, he said, "But there's always a first time. Come with me."

"Where?"

"Saint Patrick's."

We walked to the cathedral and waited by the side door until Padre Bruno, the Italian priest, made his rounds through the benches that served as pews, checking to see that the basement was empty before blowing out all the candles.

"Father," said Gaetano, "if there was a boy who lived

with a *padrone* and if the *padrone* beat the boy savagely and if that boy should happen to run away, would the church take him in?"

Padre Bruno smoothed his hands over the front of his surplice. "If there were such a boy, then there would be hundreds of such boys. If a church took one in, it would have to take all in. No church could do that." He straightened his sleeves. "And it shouldn't do it, for God, in His almighty wisdom, would take care of such a boy, if there were such a one. God has a plan for such a boy."

"God has a plan?" Gaetano bristled. "Do you really believe there's a divine plan in this boy's being beaten?"

"Yes," said Padre Bruno. "He'll come through it stronger." Even I could tell he was lying.

Gaetano looked away. When he looked back, his face had turned soft. "Please, Father, could we take clothes from the poor bin? We're not asking for charity for ourselves." He shook his head, and I shook mine, too. I didn't believe Padre Bruno was a charitable sort. "No," said Gaetano, "we want to help a family clothe their child's corpse."

For all the business smarts I had, I was a mook about how this sort of thing worked. I didn't get why Gaetano was suddenly lying. It turned out to be a perfect lie, though, because then Padre Bruno gave us an old sheet as well. For the corpse.

Walking home, Gaetano told me he wouldn't go to Saint Patrick's Cathedral anymore. He said, "A priest without faith is like a turd on a cushion. And that church is Padre Bruno's cushion."

The next morning, after the breakfast shift, we told Tin Pan Alley the plan.

"I can't run off."

"He beats you," said Gaetano.

"My *padrone* paid for me to come over from Napoli," said Tin Pan Alley. "I owe him."

"How much did the ticket cost?" I asked.

"I don't know."

"Well, I'll find out," I said. "In the meantime, you'll come live with us. When you've earned enough, you can pay your *padrone* back, if you want."

Tin Pan Alley's eyes darted around, as though he expected his *padrone* to come swooping down. "Where do you sleep?"

"What? You think we live worse than you?" Gaetano's voice shook. "Here we're ready to help, and you're insulting us."

"I just want to know," said Tin Pan Alley.

"We never lived as bad as you, even when Dom slept in a barrel," said Gaetano. "Don't you get it? You're a slave. We're free, you mook."

"I'm not a slave! You take that back."

"We have a room," I said, moving between them. "Real beds. And there's an extra one." A bubble of laughter burst from me in realization. "It's just been sitting there, for you."

"What if my *padrone* finds me? He'll beat me so bad, I won't be able to walk for days. He's done it to others."

"See these clothes?" I said. "They're yours. You'll look different."

"Clothes change nothing," said Tin Pan Alley.

"We could get you girl clothes," I said, my words coming fast. "Your *padrone* would never recognize you."

Tin Pan Alley practically gagged.

"You're nuts." Gaetano made a go-away gesture at me. "Look, Tin Pan Alley, it's not that hard," he said. "You'll just have to stay off the streets till you grow enough that he can't recognize you."

"Signora Esposito can cut his hair," I said. "That'll make him look different."

"You've got the worst ideas, Dom, do you know that?" Gaetano made that go-away gesture at me again, bigger this time. He turned to Tin Pan Alley. "I've got a barber friend. He'll cut your hair good."

"And we'll feed you," I said. "Signora Esposito cooks a lot. After a few weeks, you'll have so much flesh on your bones, he'll never guess it's you."

"What if he comes up while I'm walking away with you now?"

I looked at Gaetano. He shook out the sheet. In an instant, Tin Pan Alley understood. He climbed into the cart and curled up on his side and we covered him entirely. Then we pushed him back to Grandinetti's.

"This is my friend Tin Pan Alley. Please, can he go in your storeroom and change clothes?" I asked.

Grandinetti was busy, so he waved us through the doorway. But a few seconds later, he came into the back to get another bushel of tomatoes. Tin Pan Alley's shirt was off. When Grandinetti saw the marks on Tin Pan Alley's back, he sucked in air through his teeth. He shook his head and went back out to his customer.

After the customer left, I asked Grandinetti, "Can he spend the day here, in your store, helping out?"

Grandinetti put his palm to his forehead and sighed. I

remembered how he'd once told Gaetano and me he'd never get mixed up with a *padrone*.

He came into the storeroom, rubbed his hands with his towel, and said to Tin Pan Alley, "I'm Francesco. What's your real name, boy?"

The question took me by surprise. *Tin Pan Alley* had become his real name to me, just as *Dom* had become my real name in a way. I waited, holding my breath.

"Pietro."

"Pietro?" Grandinetti got a funny look on his face. He reached into a box, broke off a bunch of grapes, and handed them to Pietro. "You're going to have to eat a lot, if you want that flat belly to become round like the Church of San Pietro in Roma."

Gaetano and Grandinetti and I laughed. Pietro stood there a second. Then he smiled and stuffed the whole bunch of grapes in his mouth, stems and all.

Gaetano and I sold the lunch sandwiches, our eyes darting around, searching for Pietro's *padrone*. He didn't show.

That night we brought Pietro back to Signora Esposito's. She took him in without a question, but her eyes were knowing. Don't ask. Don't ask. Everyone has a past that's bad. Don't pry.

The following morning the *padrone* was waiting on Pietro's corner when we set up across the street. He stood by that same lamppost I'd first seen him at, and straightened the brim of his hat and watched us. Even though Pietro was safely back at Signora Esposito's, I shivered. When I stared at the *padrone*, Gaetano pinched me hard and told me not to look at him. But Gaetano was nervous, too; he dropped one of the egg and potato sandwiches.

The *padrone* stayed there through our morning sales. He was back again at lunch. And for the evening sales. He never said a word.

The next day he didn't come. At one point someone tapped me on the shoulder and I jumped back with a yelp. But it was just a customer.

The *padrone* didn't come back. Days passed. After a while, I stopped expecting him. I was so happy, I needed to celebrate.

One night, after dinner, when we sat on our mattresses, I pulled out the package I'd hidden under my bed. "There's something for each of you in here. But they wrapped everything in one package. Who wants to open it?"

Gaetano looked away.

Pietro looked down.

"Come on. It's a surprise. Don't you like surprises?" No one answered. What was the matter with them? "It's a celebration. Because Pietro got away from his *padrone.*"

Gaetano took the package. "Then it's for you to open, Pietro."

And I got it. I wished so much that I'd asked for two packages. Who knew when Gaetano had last had a surprise to open?

Pietro opened it carefully. He stared. And smiled.

"Shoes?" said Gaetano. He took the larger pair and turned them over in his hands. "I've never walked in shoes."

Pietro already had his on and was circling the small room. "I have," he said almost imperceptibly.

Gaetano pressed the leather with his thumb. "How'd you know the size?"

"I measured with my hand while you were sleeping."

"Who needs shoes?" But Gaetano put them on as he spoke. "How do you tie them?"

So I showed him.

Gaetano stood up. "I can wiggle my toes inside them."

Pietro laughed. "So can I."

And I realized with dismay that I couldn't anymore. My toes were cramped. My feet had grown fast. I'd have to find a way to stretch these shoes, because I was determined to wear them when I went back to Napoli. "Let's go for a walk," I said.

Pietro shook his head. "You think my *padrone*'s given up. But he hasn't. I know him. I'm not leaving this room."

"Then we can walk a hundred steps here," I said. "We can march behind one another in a circle."

"A thousand steps," said Gaetano. "And I'm in front."

After that, Gaetano wore his shoes every day. So did Pietro, though he still wouldn't leave the apartment, until one night Signora Esposito sat down on the bed beside him and slapped him on the knee and said, "Be a philosopher."

We looked at her, dumb as rocks.

"Philosophers are the smartest people around," she said, "and they don't give a fig about their appearance."

This was a little hard to listen to from a woman who powdered her face white every day. But we all wanted to know where it was leading. So we kept our eyes on her.

She got up and went to the door.

"Wait," said Pietro. "What are you talking about? I don't care what I look like."

"Then dress like a girl."

I cringed, but she didn't even look at me, so I don't think Pietro guessed that I'd told her my idea.

"Wait right there." She left and came back a few minutes later with a skirt she'd made out of an old dress. She dropped it on his lap, and she put a checkered kerchief over his hair, tying it under the chin.

As soon as she left the room, Gaetano laughed like a hyena. Pietro ripped off the kerchief. But I jabbed Gaetano with my elbow and begged Pietro to put it back on—and to wear the skirt, too. This time both Gaetano and I managed to keep a straight face.

Pietro walked a half block behind us as we went to Grandinetti's, because he was afraid that if his *padrone* saw me or Gaetano, he'd recognize Pietro, even in the skirt and kerchief, even with shoes on.

Starting that day, Pietro helped Grandinetti run the produce store. The instant he arrived at the store, he ran into the storeroom and slipped off his skirt and kerchief. Then he worked hard. He was good with money, and he was honest.

And the amazing thing was that Pietro was like a different person working beside Grandinetti. He whistled constantly. He greeted the customers and made jokes with them. And, funniest of all, he danced. At closing time, when the store was empty, he'd push the bushels back and tap and twirl. When we asked who had taught him, he clicked his heels and spun away. Over the weeks his face grew fuller and his eyes lost their haunted look.

Pietro spent money a little more easily now. One morning, as Gaetano and I were turning from Bayard onto

Mulberry Street, a Chinese boy stopped us. He was holding a big sack, and I'd seen him selling cigars on that corner before.

"Want to buy something?" said the boy in English. "Cigars? Rock candy?"

"Get away," said Gaetano in Napoletano, though there was no reason to expect the boy to understand it.

"I'll buy a piece," I said to the boy in English. I gave him two pennies and took a piece. "What else you got?"

"Domino games." The boy took out a small black box. "You play? I can teach you."

"Never heard of it," said Gaetano.

"I know how to play." Pietro came up behind us in his skirt. "Is this the Chinese game?"

"Tien Gow is too hard. This game is easy."

Pietro bought it.

When we walked on, Gaetano mumbled, *"Bastardo."*

I stiffened. "He speaks good English." Nothing I could say would irritate Gaetano more. "He never makes a mistake." I held out the brown candy. "Have some."

"Filth," said Gaetano. "Probably laced with opium."

The Chinese were known to have gambling houses where everyone smoked opium. Gaetano knew children didn't smoke it, though. He just said that sort of thing out of habit.

But even Gaetano's hatred of anyone who wasn't Italian couldn't stop him from loving dominoes. Pietro explained the game that night. We played a bunch of rounds, till one of us reached one hundred points. The low scorer was Gaetano. We played again. Gaetano won again.

"Whatever it is," Pietro said to him, "your strategy's good."

It was the first nice thing either one of them had ever said to the other.

We played almost every night after that.

After two months we felt sure that Pietro's *padrone* had given up looking for him. Another boy belonging to the same *padrone* was playing a triangle on that corner now.

The night when I told Pietro the other boy was on his corner, he stopped polishing his shoes and said, "What's he look like?" But before I could answer, he dropped his head. "No. Don't tell me." With his eyes still on the floor, he said, "Put a dollar from my share of the money into his cup."

"A dollar!" said Gaetano.

"Every day," said Pietro. "Twenty cents toward what he has to earn. And the eighty that I would have earned if I hadn't run away."

"It's your money." Gaetano got up in a huff and went to the door. "You know what? You really are a mook." He left the room.

But I understood: Pietro owed money—and you paid what you owed.

In the evenings we sometimes took walks together, Pietro in disguise and me. It was on one of those walks, on a night when the first real chill of autumn roughened our cheeks, that we did the important numbers. I'd learned that morning that a third-class ticket from Napoli to Manhattan cost between twenty and twenty-five dollars, depending on the ship. Pietro had worked for his *padrone* for more than three years, six days a week.

"At eighty cents a day," I said to Pietro, "that makes at least two hundred and fifty dollars."

Pietro's face went slack. He didn't speak.

"Come on, Pietro. You're good at numbers."

"At Signora Esposito's," he said slowly, "we each pay two dollars a week. It should cost a lot less at my *padrone*'s—he feeds us garbage. It shouldn't even cost a dollar. It shouldn't even come to fifty dollars a year."

We walked, our shoes tapping the sidewalk.

"I had no idea the passage cost so little," said Pietro. His words came faster now. "There was no one I could ask. No one any of us could ask. Our *padrone* always said it was a fortune." He put his hand over his mouth, as though he was about to be sick. Then he breathed loudly. "I've paid for my passage four or five times over. The boys I lived with—almost all of them have paid over and over."

"And the thief beat you."

"He beat all of us," said Pietro.

"You don't owe him. You're free."

"I'm free," said Pietro, but his voice was small.

"Don't be sad," I said. "It's over. That part of your life is behind. Now you've really got a reason to dance."

"Gaetano was right all along; I'm a mook."

"Don't say that."

Pietro looked at me and his eyes glistened in the light of the streetlamp. "I lied just now. I could have found out the price of a ticket if I'd really wanted to. But I was afraid of being on my own. I hated my *padrone*—but I stayed with him." He turned his face away and wiped his cheek. "And he counted on that. He counted on our being more afraid of freedom than of him."

"You're not afraid anymore."

"Because I have you now. You're my friend."

"So is Gaetano."

"I know," said Pietro. "And you're both braver than me. I couldn't do it alone, like you did."

I put my hand on his shoulder. "Let's go home and write to your aunt."

"My aunt. She said she'd never leave Napoli. But maybe if I sent her the money, she would."

"Let's go."

"I've got to think about this first," said Pietro. "You go on ahead." He walked up Mulberry Street slowly.

I didn't go home. Instead, I went down to the wharves almost without realizing where I was going. I stood at the black water. A huge passenger ship was docked there. For I don't know how long, I'd been telling myself it was time to find out about the cost of a ticket. One thousand sandwiches had come and gone long before. I'd stopped counting, but we'd probably sold two thousand by now. Every day I shoved my fist in my shoes, trying to stretch them, and I told myself to go find out. But I kept putting it off. I'd been too busy. I still went over my Napoli memories every night, to keep them sharp. And they still made me feel better. But I was so busy, I didn't think about Italy much during the day—not much at all—hardly ever.

And maybe it wasn't just because I was busy. Maybe it was also because I liked our business. I loved it. And I loved Gaetano and Pietro and Grandinetti and even Signora Esposito.

Now I was dazed to think I had far more than enough

money saved for a boat ticket. And no matter how much phony documents cost, I probably had plenty for them, too. I could go back to Napoli anytime I chose.

The water lapped around the ship quietly. I stared at moonlight on black water.

CHAPTER TWENTY-ONE

Crosby Street

I should have been overjoyed to know I could go back. I walked slowly, reminding myself of what I loved about my city. Going over my memories usually made me feel safe. As long as I did that, nothing truly awful could happen.

But it didn't work that night: when I got home, Pietro wasn't there.

He didn't come back and he didn't come back.

Even inside, I grew so cold, my teeth ached.

At midnight Gaetano said, "Go to bed. I'll look for him."

Instead, I went out the door with him.

We walked up and down every street and every alley of Five Points, calling his name softly so we wouldn't wake anyone. Pietro wouldn't have left the neighborhood. He was still far too skittish to do that. Wasn't he?

We went back home at dawn, just the two of us.

A sense of dread made me sluggish. I'd seen life change in a flash. One moment I was Mamma's boy; the next I was on my own. But this couldn't be another flash. I wouldn't let it. Pietro had to come back.

We couldn't search anymore. Not now. It was a work-day, and people depended on us. Old Lady Cassone would have egg and potato sandwiches waiting in less than an hour. And there were Pierano and Grandinetti and Witold, the Polish butcher, and Martino, the baker, and the boys, Michele and Nicola and Roberto, who wanted to sell from the cart—all of them counting on us.

So we went to work.

As we were selling breakfast, I looked over at the boy playing the triangle. I'd looked at him every chance I got all morning, but he'd always had his back to me, as though on purpose. Now I caught him looking at me, too. He turned his back instantly.

Something awful had happened for sure.

Pietro had talked about the *padrone*'s other boys the night before. He'd said almost all of them had paid their debt over and over. He'd said none of them knew that.

Everything outside my head went silent. Pietro was loyal. He'd never let those other boys stay in the dark about this.

I walked up to the boy.

His eyes showed terror and he turned his back to me.

"Is he at your *padrone*'s place?" I asked, speaking to his back.

He played his triangle loud and fast.

"Okay," I said. "I don't want to get you in trouble. I need information, that's all. You live on Crosby Street—I know that much. Just tell me the number."

He played that triangle as though his life depended on it.

Maybe it did.

I walked away fast, looking around, praying his *padrone* wasn't spying.

As we pushed the cart back to Five Points to get ready for the lunch shift, I asked Gaetano, "Did Pietro ever tell you where his *padrone* lives?"

"No. And don't even think about it."

"He told me he lived on Crosby Street, but I don't know where exactly."

"Shut up!" said Gaetano.

"He went there. I'm almost sure of it. I told you what he said when he found out how much a ticket costs. He went to tell the other boys."

"Shut up! I mean it." Gaetano grabbed both handles of the cart and pushed fast.

I ran along beside him. "He told me once that his *padrone* ties the boys to the bedposts at night so they won't run away. He's probably tied up right now."

"It doesn't matter. I know what the *padroni* do. Everyone in Five Points knows. Everyone but you. We've all seen it. You can't do anything to help him."

"Yes, I can!"

Bam! And I was on the ground, my ear ringing where Gaetano had punched me.

"Shut up! No crazy plans!" he shouted down at me. "You don't know what happened to him. You don't know anything, you mook. And even if you're right, it's his own fault for going there. Anything you do might get you in trouble and you'll be dead, or good as dead. It'll be so bad that you'll wish you were dead. So just shut up!" He wiped his eyes with the back of one hand and went back to pushing the cart.

I got to my feet and punched Gaetano in the middle of his back.

He whirled around and put up his fists. But then he shook his head and dropped them.

We went through the motions of the lunch shift almost without thinking. But after lunch, all I could see was Pietro, hanging in the wind. Abandoned. Nonna would have been so ashamed of me. Loyalty was everything. Pietro's *padrone* was bad—the way Franco on the cargo ship was bad. When Franco kept Mamma off the ship, I didn't do anything because I didn't know what was going on. But now . . . I couldn't stand this!

Gaetano could handle the evening shift without me. All he had to do was try to speak English, and he could do the whole thing with a couple of boys helping him.

So while Gaetano was off buying the candies to load on the cart, I put one of the last oranges of the season in my pocket for Pietro and I ran up Mulberry to Canal Street and asked which way Crosby was.

I was there in five minutes. The trouble was, Crosby Street was lined on both sides with tall buildings. And it was long. Pietro could have been tied up in any one of hundreds of apartments.

Well. There was still a couple of hours, at least, before the boys who worked for the *padrone* would come home. So the *padrone* himself was out on the streets, checking up on them. If I went fast, if I had any kind of luck, I'd find Pietro in that time.

The first building had a laundry on the ground floor. I went up one flight. Then the second. Then the third. I knocked on door after door. At a few, no one answered. Two were opened by women. Two by old men. One by a group of children. The children slammed the door in my face. Most adults shooed me away. One woman answered, but she didn't know where a *padrone* and a bunch of children lived. But one old man said, "There's a *padrone* in every building, the whole length of Crosby."

How many *padroni* could there be in this city? Dozens? Hundreds? But I couldn't think like that. The search was just starting.

I tried the next building. And the one after that. So many doors. Confused faces. Frightened. Annoyed.

I was coming down from the top floor of the sixth building when I heard a woman singing, *"Daisy, Daisy, give me your answer do. I'm half crazy . . ."* I stopped and gripped the banister. A second later I was face to face with Pietro's *padrone*, climbing the stairs. Our eyes met in a moment of shock; then his face twisted with rage. I turned and ran back up the stairs and down the hall to the door at the end, the only door on that floor where someone had answered me—an elderly woman, but at least she had a lock on her door. Before I got there, he hooked me around the chest from behind. He clamped his other hand over my mouth.

Caught! And good as dead.

I tried to bite, I kicked, I reached my hands over my head and scratched at his eyes. He lugged me to the rear

223

apartment. Then he let go of my chest and twisted one arm up behind me till I saw stars.

"If you make a noise, I'll pull your arm out of the socket," he spat in my ear. "You haven't known pain till you've felt that. Then I'll throw you out the back window. Understand?" He kept hold of my arm and took his other hand off my mouth and fumbled with a key in the lock.

I screamed.

He had the door open and shoved me through so hard, I fell and skidded halfway across the floor, dizzy and sick. But he'd let go of my arm.

He locked the door behind him and stood there.

I breathed deep, getting ready to shout my lungs out. When he came at me, I'd have to move fast and grab anything I could use as a weapon.

He stood there.

So I let my eyes take in the room. Along the wall to my left were iron rings with rope through them. A small boy lay on his side in the corner, one wrist tied to the last ring. His eyes were closed, but I thought I saw his eyelids move. Pietro had lied; the boys weren't bound to bedposts—there were no beds. They lay on the floor, like animals.

The table near the door held stacks of bowls and a pile of spoons. Beside it a hook stuck out from the wall. A short whip curled on it. On the other side of the table was a single chair. The *padrone* dropped his hat on that chair.

And he just stood there.

My eyes jumped across him to the wall with windows looking out the rear of the building. Beside a large wood trunk stood an old three-drawer bureau. The bottom drawer was partway open. There was a single bed and a large wood crate full of ratty blankets, and another crate overflowing with clothes.

"Why . . . ," came the gruff voice. The *padrone* cleared his throat. "Why are you here?" he asked, now in a more normal tone, speaking Napoletano. The rage was gone from his face. Everything was gone from his face.

Caught and good as dead.

I had nothing to lose.

"Where's Pietro?" I said loudly.

The boy in the corner let out a little hiss, as though he'd touched a hot stove. I looked at him and he rolled over to face the wall. He was so skinny that his hip bone smacked on the floor as he moved. He stuck the index finger of his free hand in his top ear and pressed the other ear into the floor.

"There's no Pietro here."

"He came here last night," I said.

The *padrone*'s eyes flickered for a second. "You looked around just now. You didn't find him. Why?" He picked up his hat and sat on the chair and leaned toward me. "Because he isn't here," he growled.

"I won't leave without him."

One side of the *padrone*'s top lip curled up at that. "Did your *padrone* send you to take his place?"

"His place isn't here," I said. "He doesn't owe you a thing. He paid off his debt years ago. Most of the boys did. A passage only costs twenty-five dollars. They just don't know it."

The *padrone* jumped to his feet.

I flinched, ready to spring out of the way. And I gasped. Just tensing my muscles like that hurt my shoulder so bad.

"You're lucky my boy here is sick and isn't listening," he said. "I won't have my boys infected with your nonsense."

"You're a criminal." I made my voice as strong as I could. "Everything you do is illegal."

He jammed his hat on and felt around the rim with both hands, slowly. "So you're not a criminal? You've got a *padrone*, that makes you part of the crime, too. Or, hey, don't you have a *padrone*? Huh?"

How stupid I'd been to say that. If anything could have protected me, it was a *padrone*. "I have a boss."

"A boss, huh?" He pointed at me. "Well, your boss broke the rules. He stole my boy. He owes me." He stuck out his bottom lip. "He owes me you. And with training, I think you'll make a good worker." He lunged and grabbed me by the shoulder that was still throbbing, holding me at arm's length. With the other hand he took the whip and lashed. My back was aflame. He struck again and again, till I was hanging from his hand. Then he dragged me to the wall and dropped me facedown and bound my wrist to an iron ring. "The rest of the lesson will have to wait. The boys will be home soon. I have to go pick up their supper. You'll wait for me." And he left, locking the door behind him.

My mouth was open in the scream I never let out. It was easier to breathe that way. There was no limit to my pain, fire all over my back. I knew I was bleeding, and bad. The tatters of my shirt stuck to me, even on my belly.

Gaetano had been right. I almost wished I was dead.

The boy rolled over toward me. His face was flushed and feverish.

I forced myself onto my side and pushed my bound arm as close to him as I could. "Can you help me? With your free hand and mine, we can untie the rope."

"He'll catch you. Then it'll be worse."

"He won't catch me. Help me. Please."

"If you get away, he'll kill me."

"Come with me."

"I don't want to."

"Okay," I said in desperation. "Okay, you can say I had a knife. You can say I cut myself loose."

"Do you have a knife?"

"No."

The boy shut his eyes.

"Where's Pietro?" I asked.

"How do you know him?"

I worked my pocket open. The orange was still there. "This is for him." I put it on the floor in front of the boy's nose. "He's my friend."

The boy struggled to a sitting position. "He's my friend, too." He bit the orange that was for Pietro, chewing the peel and all. "There's a knife in the top drawer of the bureau." He took another bite. "If we get you free, you have to cut the rope and put the knife back. Then the *padrone* will believe me that you had a knife."

"Okay."

"You swear on the Virgin Mary?"

The Virgin Mary wasn't anyone to me. But I would do what the boy said. "I swear."

"Say it. Say 'I swear on the Virgin Mary.' "

"I swear on the Virgin Mary."

We worked at that knot. The boy's fingers were better

at it—stronger—mine trembled so. The knot came loose at last. "Thank you."

I crawled across the floor to the bureau, pulled open the top drawer, crawled back with the knife, and cut the rope.

The boy looked beyond me and his face showed horror.

I looked, too. A telltale trail of blood ran to the bureau and back. Even the knife was bloody. Everything I had touched was bloody. I got to my feet with difficulty and took a shirt off the top of the pile of clothes in the open crate.

A shoe tumbled to the floor. One of Pietro's shoes. I looked at the boy, tears already dropping hot on my hands.

"He's dead," he said. "My *padrone* beat him till he died."

Something inside me creaked high and thin, as though I was coming apart. "Come with me," I managed.

"I can't."

"You have to."

"My brother is here. If I leave, my brother will pay."

Caught and good as dead.

I used the shirt to wipe the blood off the handle of the knife, then put the knife back in the bureau and shut the drawer and wiped the bureau. Then I mopped up the trail of blood.

I searched in the crate for Pietro's other shoe. Got it. "Where's his body?"

"I don't know," said the boy. "But there are two rivers."

I couldn't manage the stairs holding those shoes. So I threw them down a flight. Then I clung to the rickety banister. The world kept getting dark. There was no window in the hall, but I knew it was more than that—I was fighting to stay conscious. Down a flight. I picked up the shoes and threw them before me again. Down another flight. I threw the shoes the last flight, and as they left my hand, I fell, tumbling head over heels, my back blazing.

I lay at the bottom of the stairwell and looked toward the door to the street. It was only a body's length away. But I couldn't do it. I couldn't.

Survive.

Mamma's first rule.

Simply survive.

I rolled onto my stomach and pulled my arms in under my chest and tried to push myself to sitting. I couldn't.

Pietro's shoes had landed off to the side. He had loved those shoes as much as I loved mine. But it would take so much energy to get them.

Survive.

I dragged myself to the door. With every last bit of strength I had, I grabbed the knob and pulled myself to my feet, and I fell through the door as it opened, out onto the sidewalk.

That's when I heard them. "Dom!" they were yelling. "Dom! Dom, where are you?" And then, "Look! That's him." And the sound of running. Shoes running. Two sets. I wanted to see them, both of them. I wanted to tell them to save Pietro's shoes. But I blacked out.

CHAPTER TWENTY-TWO

Eldridge Street

Gaetano once said that a few days alone was enough to make a kid grow up. I didn't know if that was true. But that night in the *padrone*'s room, I grew up for sure.

Grandinetti reported the *padrone* to the police, but no one expected anything to come of it. Boys disappeared all the time. There were way too many cases for the police to follow up on. Boys were dispensable.

The worst thing was, it was my fault Pietro died. I was the one who came up with the idea of his escape. Gaetano helped against his better judgment. Grandinetti and Signora Esposito were pulled in out of decency. But I started it.

Gaetano never reproached me. Grandinetti and Signora Esposito never reproached me.

And Pietro—I couldn't imagine Pietro ever reproaching me for anything.

Friends forgave.

How terrible it was to need such forgiveness.

I stayed at home for days while Gaetano and Grandinetti ran the business. They took Pietro's death as hard as I did. But I was the one with the ripped-up back. Signora Esposito bought ice to glide over my back and neck. All I could do was lie there and think. I hadn't saved Pietro's shoes. If I could have done it all over again, I'd have grabbed them. I'd have found the energy somehow.

But now there was nothing I could do for him. I couldn't even write to his aunt to tell her he had died. I knew the street—Vico Sedil Capuano—but I had never found out Pietro's last name. And maybe the aunt had a different last name, anyway. There was nothing I could do for his spirit.

As soon as I could put a shirt on without gasping in pain, I went out to Baxter Street, to Witold, the Polish butcher.

He greeted me with a big smile. "Welcome back, my friend," he said in halting English. "You went missing."

Guilt stabbed me. I hadn't asked Gaetano anything about the business since the night the *padrone* had whipped me. "No one came to buy beef from you?"

"Oh, yes, yes, my friend. Another boy comes. Every day."

I let out my breath in relief. Good old Gaetano. I could imagine his hating every moment of it. But he did it. For the business.

"In fact, he has already come today. I am sorry you wasted your time coming here."

231

"I came for a different reason. I want to go to synagogue with you."

Witold laced his fingers together on his belly. "You understand Hebrew?"

"I remember some."

He looked at me for a full minute, I was sure. Then he nodded gravely. "You are just what America needs—just what has been lacking—an Italian Jew."

I blinked.

He laughed. "Come back at six. You can eat with my family beforehand."

Oh, it was Friday. I hadn't even realized. I'd come in time for the Sabbath. As I walked out, I reached up and touched the *mezuzah*. I was tall enough now to do it without a boost.

That evening Witold's family ate sour cabbage. I had to fight to keep my nose from wrinkling. They spoke fast, with so many harsh sounds in a row.

"Polish must be a hard language," I said.

They laughed. "That wasn't Polish," said Witold. "That was Yiddish—what Eastern European Jews speak. Some just call it Jewish."

I felt stupid. Italian Jews didn't speak Yiddish. I couldn't begin to mimic them. What was I doing there?

But then Witold's wife draped an old sweater over my shoulders and told me I could keep it. And Witold put a yarmulke on my head. And everything was right again. I felt small. Like before Mamma put me on that cargo ship. Safe.

Witold wrapped himself in his prayer shawl and the family walked east on Canal Street to the synagogue on

Eldridge Street. With every step I could feel the new scabs on my back crack open, setting me on fire all over again. But I kept my eyes on the white tassels of that prayer shawl and tried to listen as Witold told me about the history of the synagogue. It was new, built only in 1887. Anyone was welcome, but, really, it was an Eastern European synagogue. The rabbi spoke Yiddish, after all.

The service was long, and my back hurt so much I could barely listen to the Hebrew. I hardly knew Hebrew, anyway. But I was there, in the Most Powerful One's house. I was begging His forgiveness, His mercy on my wretchedness. I cried, the way I'd cried when I found Pietro's shoe at the *padrone*'s, silently.

Over the next week, day by day, my strength came back. I kept that yarmulke in my pocket and the following Friday afternoon I went back to Witold with a bottle of Falanghina—wine from Napoli.

Witold put the bottle on one end of his butcher counter. I tilted my head in question. "I do not drink," he said. "But it makes good decoration. An Italian gift from my Italian friend."

I set the yarmulke on my head and ate stinky food with his chattering family and went off to synagogue with Poles and Russians. I didn't understand much of anything.

Beniamino—Dom—it didn't matter what I was called. I was Napoletano, and I didn't belong at an Eastern European service. I couldn't just worm my way into Witold's world and the comfort of his community. I couldn't pretend that all this was mine.

It wasn't a synagogue that made a Jew, anyway. It wasn't a yarmulke or a *mezuzah*. I was Jewish inside. In my head.

I had to use that head like Mamma said, to find my own way to be loyal to everything that mattered to me. That was the only way to survive, and *Survive* was her first rule.

When I explained to Witold, he put his hands on my shoulders and said, "Shalom, my friend."

Shalom. Peace.

I hadn't thought of myself as being in a battle. But Witold was right—war raged inside me. I wanted to scream half the time.

I wanted to scream because the idea of going back to Napoli had died. I no longer yearned for it, though I still spent the last hour before falling asleep trying to smell the scents of every corner of our home in Napoli, trying to feel every swatch of material, to taste every sauce in every pot. This was my private treasure.

But maybe the lion statues at the Piazza dei Martiri weren't as large as I remembered. Maybe Palazzo Sessa, the synagogue, wasn't that high. Maybe Mamma wasn't sitting in a window crying for me.

It didn't matter anyway, because I wasn't going back.

In December I'd turn ten. I'd have a little celebration with Gaetano and Grandinetti and Signora Esposito, and maybe even some of the boys who worked for us at the cart. They'd say, *"Cent'anni,"* wishing me one hundred years of healthy life. One hundred years away from Napoli. One hundred years without Mamma.

That made me want to scream, because so long as I planned to return to Napoli, I had something to work for.

I didn't belong in Napoli anymore.

Mamma didn't want me there. It hurt so bad to know

that. But I couldn't stop the knowing anymore. Gaetano had helped me to know. My friend Gaetano.

And my friend Pietro, he had helped me, too. He had said something that last time we were together. He'd said he could have found out the price of a passage—but he didn't want to. He was more afraid of being alone than of his *padrone*. He was a liar. Like me.

I remembered Mamma's words to Franco. I had lied to myself about that. I remembered them exactly, because I'd stood there that morning and wanted to ask her why she kept talking about my going—why she hadn't talked about our going.

Mamma put me on that ship alone on purpose. My mamma did that terrible thing to me. I couldn't pretend I didn't know anymore.

And now I belonged here.

I remembered Uncle Aurelio saying a true Napoletano couldn't stay away forever. That was why when the Jews were sent out of Napoli, they kept sneaking back. But I could. I could stay in Five Points forever.

I had a life here, and a family of sorts. It wasn't the family I was born into. But I loved them. No one in this new family had betrayed me. I belonged with them—that was what going to Witold's synagogue had taught me. My family was that comfort I needed.

Pietro was wrong: I wasn't any braver than he was. I couldn't face what Mamma had done on my own. It took my new family to help me.

And the business, too. That kept me working and feeling useful. By now the brothers who had worked for our cart all summer had left us to go to school. Their family didn't send them to parochial school, even though they were Catholic, because the Irish ran those schools and no Italians wanted their children acting like the Irish. So they went to Public School 23 over on City Hall Place. I'd see them walking there in the morning. It wasn't far. I knew, because I followed them once. It was just between Duane and Pearl streets.

So we had been hiring other boys—older ones who had already dropped out of school. Some were new immigrants who had tried school, but because they couldn't speak English, they were put in the primary grades. They hated being with babies and being forced to speak English badly in front of their classmates. Plenty of them weren't fresh off the boat, though. They had come to America really young and stayed in school through the second grade, at least. But even as little guys, they couldn't take being made fun of for their English. So they quit.

Older boys cost us more than the brothers had. Some of them didn't like taking orders from Gaetano. And they hated taking orders from me. They pocketed money and stole food.

One day when Grandinetti was listening to me and Gaetano complain about the thefts, he said, "What do you love about working?"

"What?" said Gaetano. "No one loves working."

"You do. You love this business. Both of you."

"Well, the business," said Gaetano. "Sure, I'm happy with the business."

"Tell me why."

Gaetano held out his hands. "It's simple. We make money."

"You could make money in a factory job," said Grandinetti.

"Not as much," said Gaetano. "Besides, I'd hate it."

"Me too," I said. "Someone else would tell us what to do all the time."

"*Appunto!* Exactly." Grandinetti pointed at me. "Okay, so maybe you've got to give these boys more responsibility. More authority."

"Never," said Gaetano. "We decide what happens with our cart."

But I saw what Grandinetti meant. "We could buy a second cart."

"What are you talking about?" said Gaetano. "That's got nothing to do with anything."

"I'd stay with one cart, you'd stay with the other."

"What? Compete with each other? Are you nuts?"

"I'd set up on a different corner, a few blocks away."

"But who would speak to the customers at my cart?"

"Come on, Gaetano. You know you can speak English."

His temples pulsed.

"You're such a hardhead." I threw up my hands. "You know you can do it. And you can do the numbers, too. You're fast at adding now."

"How would it solve anything? We'd both need helpers then. We'd double our problems."

"We'd take partners—maybe Umberto and Emilio. They're smart. And they'd watch out that their friends didn't steal. People aren't going to steal from a friend anyway."

"I can't believe you'd say that," said Gaetano. "You'll die a mook, you know that?"

"I'll die the king of Mulberry Street."

Grandinetti laughed. "I believe you will, Dom."

"Because, look, we'd pool the money from both carts," I said, without slowing down, "and earn more."

"Double," said Gaetano. "We'll earn double."

"Well . . . see, that's the point of having partners. The carts would pull in double, but we'd each make the same, because our new partners would share. Twenty-five percent for each of us, because we'd all be equal."

"Whoa. We don't need more partners."

"Sure we do. We'll have double the number of sandwiches to buy and cut up and rewrap. Double the work. They have to be partners, too."

"I don't know, Dom. We'd have to get along with them. Pay attention to what they think. It could ruin us."

"We paid attention to what Pietro thought—and we did good. We did better because of him." My whole body went hot. "Pietro was proud to be a partner," I said softly. "Let's give Umberto and Emilio a chance."

"Wait a minute," said Gaetano. "Wait just one minute." He looked away. He walked around Grandinetti's store. He rubbed above his mouth at the thin mustache that anyone could see now. "No."

"But . . ."

"No. You and I get thirty percent each. They get twenty each. Until we see how it works out." He grinned. "And I get Emilio on my cart."

238

By December both carts were doing all right, and nobody stole from us.

It was almost Christmas. On the weekends I took walks and eavesdropped on passing conversations. No one could stop talking about their mother, it seemed. About what she always cooked for the holidays, about her every ache and pain, about how she should have been named Maria (if she wasn't) after the Virgin Mary. There's a Napoletano proverb that goes, *"Mamma e giuventù s'apprezzano quanno nun se teneno chiù"*—Your mother and your youth you appreciate only when they're gone. But it's not true. Italians love their mother every day of their lives, and especially at Christmastime.

This wasn't my holiday. Hanukah happened around now; I didn't know exactly when. But my birthday was coming, so I thought I'd buy myself a present.

Vendors had set up tables all along Mulberry Street with nativity scenes, just like the ones down Via dei Tribunali in Napoli. I walked up and down, looking over the tiny wire baskets filled with clay eggs and the minuscule paper bags overflowing with ceramic apples—all just like in Napoli. And I smiled to realize that it was a true memory. I'd forgotten about these scenes. But I remembered now.

Then Signora Esposito got a letter from her daughter, who lived way across the country in San Francisco, California. She couldn't read it, so I read it to her. And she praised me to the skies. She brought her friends to me so I could read the letters they got from relatives during the holidays. I was just like Uncle Vittorio, reading letters to the women. And that was a true memory, too. I used to want to get a letter from someone who loved me—and to write a letter to someone I loved. I remembered that.

And now I couldn't stop the memories. The way a woman held her baby reminded me of Aunt Sara and Baby Daniela. The way another woman lugged two large bottles of wine, one in each hand, reminded me of Aunt Rebecca. And, yes, the way a woman stopped and squatted in front of her son and smoothed his shirt reminded me of Mamma.

I couldn't keep myself from remembering Mamma. A woman tucking a towel over a basket of produce was Mamma tucking the sheet over me to keep out mosquitoes. A woman tapping a winter melon to see if it was ripe was Mamma tapping me on the head for coming home late. That woman running her hands through her hair as she stood wistfully in front of a flower store was Mamma—and that one swinging a package in one hand and holding tight to a child's hand in the other was Mamma—and that one throwing her shawl proudly over her shoulders was Mamma. Mamma everywhere, in everyone. Even Signora Esposito frying meatballs became Mamma.

Christmas Eve was a Saturday. I walked through the last-minute shoppers, my feet pinched in those well-worn shoes. People's breath puffed out in front of them. I couldn't remember seeing breath like that before; Napoli got cold, but not this cold. It was as though our souls danced in front of our lips.

I buttoned my jacket and headed for Mott Street, for the shoe store where I'd bought Pietro's and Gaetano's shoes. It was already early evening, so the Sabbath was over. I bought a pair of shoes with plenty of room, and I put my old ones in the box, and I went outside and lost myself in the crowd again. I walked and walked.

The shoes Mamma gave me had saved me so many times. Without them, I might have been thrown in an orphanage after I was fished out of the water that first day in America. Without them, the translators at Ellis Island would have let that "uncle" claim me for the *padrone* he worked for. Without them, I wouldn't have been able to borrow twenty-five cents from Grandinetti to buy that first sandwich to cut up and sell. Mamma did a smart thing in buying those shoes for me—it was probably the smartest thing she could have done. And I knew she'd sacrificed to do it, maybe in ways that were awful. She'd tried to protect me, even though she was crazy to put me on the boat. She'd tried. Those shoes were the proof.

I'd been walking for half an hour, up and down the streets. I'd been ready to be disappointed with my new shoes. Instead, with each step they felt better. They felt wonderful. In an instant I knew: Pietro's spirit lived in these shoes, just like my grandfather's spirit lived in the credenza in our home in Napoli.

I stopped and looked down and made a promise to Pietro's spirit about what I'd do in these shoes. I'd find a way to fight the *padroni*—to fight the whole *padrone* system. I had no idea how, but I'd do it. I walked on with determination.

Somehow I found myself on Eldridge Street, passing by Witold's synagogue. But I didn't stop. I walked north, block after block, enjoying my new shoes. The street was empty here, except for a boy, maybe six or seven years old, who stood on the sidewalk, his feet ghostly on the freezing pavement, and peeked through a lit window. I stopped beside him and looked in.

The room was full of people standing in groups, drinking and eating and laughing.

"What's going on?" I asked the boy in Napoletano.

He looked at me briefly; then his eyes went back to the party scene inside.

"What is this?" I asked, this time in English.

He shook his head and said something in a language with a lot of rough sounds.

I walked over to the door. The sign on it read NEIGHBORHOOD GUILD. I'd heard about this place. It was one of the new settlement houses that gave English lessons. Those people inside were probably all immigrants, celebrating the holiday with their classmates.

I went back to the boy and looked through the window with him. Maybe that overweight man was his father. Or maybe the balding man. Or maybe the one missing a front tooth. Or maybe none of them.

I handed the boy my shoe box. "Happy Hanukah." I smiled. "Merry Christmas."

The boy blinked at me. He said something in his strange language, turned tail, and ran. A block away he stopped to open the box. He looked back at me and waved.

I grinned and waved hard.

Who could tell what that boy might do in those shoes.

I thought of my promise to Pietro to fight the *padroni*. To do that, I'd have to go to school and get the education Mamma wanted for me. I could start with night classes at the settlement house.

My cheeks were wet. White stuck to my eyelashes. White bits sparkled in the air. Snow! My first snowfall, dusting the world.

I walked home to Signora Esposito's, leaving sharp footprints behind me in that perfect white. When I went into the kitchen, she was humming and grinding nuts to layer on fettuccine with cinnamon and powdered sugar—a sweet dish, my favorite. She was making all the best dishes for my birthday dinner. I kissed her on the cheek.

She smiled softly and kept on humming.

POSTSCRIPT

This is a fictional story that takes place in 1892. I have dedicated it to Thad Guyer, my wonderful friend, who started me on the road to being a writer, and to the spirits of my grandfathers.

My maternal grandfather was born Rosario Grandinetti, but when he came to the United States from Calabria, Italy (leaving through the port at Napoli on the ship *Bolivia*), he was called Francesco or Frank. He was a housepainter and he died before I was born. Everything I have ever heard about him makes me think he had a spirit like that of the produce vendor in this story.

My paternal grandfather went by various names over his lifetime, too, but his name as given on my father's birth certificate was Domenico Napolillo. His place of birth, according to that certificate, was simply Italy, but my father said he spoke a variety of the Neapolitan dialect. And my cousin Valerie says he came from Positano. He was born on December 24, 1888. During the years that I knew him, he went by the name Dan J. Napoli. My father told me the *J* was for James, but my mother told me the *J* was just because he liked it. (There is no letter *J* in standard Italian words; *J* occurs in foreign words and sometimes in words from Italian dialects.)

My mother told me that Domenico came to America alone as a stowaway when he was only five years old. She told me this years after both my father and grandfather had died. My cousin Valerie heard the same story from her mother, my father's sister. My other relatives seem to have varying and somewhat vague stories about him. Unfortunately, I have been unable to find any legal documents concerning my paternal grandfather other than my own father's birth certificate.

But everyone agrees that he was an illegitimate child who started out penniless. And that he became a successful businessman quite young. My father told me stories of how Domenico started a business as a sandwich vendor in New York when he was just a child. He bought long sandwiches in Five Points for twenty-five cents, cut them into quarters, and sold them on Wall Street for twenty-five cents each. Soon he had many other children working for him.

The events in this story, however, are more informed by my reading of histories of Napoli and New York and old magazines and newspapers, and by my looking at old photographs, and by my spending long days wandering both cities, than by my parents' anecdotes. I wish very much that it were otherwise. When my grandfather was alive, I had little interest in his history. What I wouldn't give to be able to sit down with him today and simply listen.

ABOUT THE AUTHOR

Donna Jo Napoli is the author of many distinguished books for young readers, among them *The Great God Pan, Daughter of Venice, Crazy Jack, The Magic Circle, Zel, Sirena, Breath, Bound,* and *Stones in Water.* She has a BA in mathematics and a PhD in Romance linguistics from Harvard University and has taught widely at major universities in America and abroad. She lives with her family in Swarthmore, Pennsylvania, where she is a professor of linguistics at Swarthmore College.